For Beth Hummel Waas,
our faithful baby-sitter and friend.
Thanks for loving us
in spite of our shenanigans!

THE NEVER-ENDING DAY
Copyright © 1997 by Lissa Halls Johnson
All rights reserved. International copyright secured.

Library of Congress Cataloging-in-Publication Data
Johnson, Lissa Halls, 1955-
    The never-ending day / Lissa Halls Johnson.
        p. cm. — (China Tate series; #7)
    Summary: When China and Deedee agree to babysit for six ram-
bunctious brothers and sisters instead of going on a weekend house-
boating trip, they wonder why God makes some choices so difficult.
    ISBN 1-56179-538-0
    [1. Babysitters—Fiction. 2. Brothers and sisters—Fiction.
3. Christian life—Fiction. 4. Camps—Fiction.] I. Title. II Series:
Johnson, Lissa Halls, 1955- China Tate series; 7.
PZ7.J63253Ne   1997
[Fic]—dc21   97-6251
Printed in the United States of America   CIP
                                                       AC

Published by Focus on the Family Publishing,
Colorado Springs, Colorado 80995.
Distributed in the U.S.A. and Canada by Word Books, Dallas, Texas.

Editor: Deena Davis
Cover Design: Big Cat Inc (BC Studios)
Cover Illustration: Matt Duncan

97 98 99 00/10 9 8 7 6 5 4 3 2 1

CHAPTER ONE

CHINA TATE PLACED HER HANDS on the armrests and imagined the heavy straps on an execution chair being buckled over her wrists. While someone fastened the ankle restraints, another person buckled straps around her knees.

In only moments her executioner would receive the final go-ahead, and China's life would be over.

Mr. Kiersey, her best friend's father and the camp director of Camp Crazy Bear, had summoned her to his office only once before. And that was when Heather Hamilton, jealous of China's friendship with Deedee Kiersey, had lied, hoping to get China sent home. Heather told Mr. Kiersey that China had stolen the camp's boat rental money. China was almost sent to her Aunt Liddy's in disgrace. To China, this office, and especially this chair, represented fear, humiliation, and despair. She shut her eyes, waiting for the helmet to be snapped in place over her head.

What is my crime? she wondered silently.

She wished Mr. Kiersey would get off the phone and

1

get it over with. *He's going to send me home this time,* she thought. *I'm a bad influence on Deedee. I cost too much to feed. I'm too much trouble.* China swallowed around the lump in her throat. Nothing she did was ever right. She managed to turn even the simplest things into gargantuan disasters. Would she ever be able to walk two steps without causing something to go wrong?

Mr. Kiersey laughed into the phone and winked at China. "I understand completely, Mr. Macon. Magda says she has an idea. I'll let her talk to you about it."

China closed her ears to the conversation. After the "murder" plot she and Deedee had overheard earlier that summer, she knew better than to eavesdrop. Her fertile mind could be a dangerous thing; it took simple idea seeds and made beanstalks out of them.

She wished Deedee were here. Deedee would at least try to calm her by reminding her for the tenth time that her dad never called anyone to his office unless it had to do with work. That was sort of calming. But then, if this meeting had to do with work, she must be in big trouble. But everything had been going smoothly in the kitchen. Besides, why wouldn't Magda come directly to her if there were a problem? Or Rick?

China was so lost in thought that she didn't hear Mr. Kiersey hang up the phone.

"China," Mr. Kiersey said, startling her, "I have some bad news for you." He started to press his fingers together. When he did that, China always thought it looked like a spider doing push-ups on a mirror.

She stared at his hands, afraid to look at his eyes. She hoped she wouldn't cry when he told her she had to go home.

Mr. Kiersey sighed. "You've been doing a great job in the camp kitchen. Magda loves you. You're a hard worker."

It was China's turn to sigh. *But I'm just a lousy worker overall, right? It's that tray of bread I put in the oven and forgot about until the smoke alarm went off.*

"This morning we received word that a new law has been passed," he said.

China wrinkled her forehead. *A law? What in the world does that have to do with me?*

"I know you will think this is all your fault." Mr. Kiersey locked eyes with China. "It's only because of the law."

China started to fidget. If it were Deedee on the other side of the desk, China would have demanded she spit it out by now. China pressed her lips together so she wouldn't say something to get herself in trouble.

"The law states that you have to be 18 years old or older to work in a large industrial kitchen such as ours."

China dropped her head to one side and scrunched up her nose. "Why?" she asked.

Mr. Kiersey picked up a pencil and started to tap it

on the desk. China waited for him to speak. "It must be that someone somewhere sued one too many times about getting injured."

"Or maybe," China said, "they figure all 15-year-olds are a little berserk and will attack the cook in a moment of hormonal rage."

Mr. Kiersey smiled.

China leaned forward as if involving Mr. Kiersey in a conspiracy. "I wonder if Dr. Hamilton had something to do with this law. . . ." She thought of Heather's father, an arrogant trauma surgeon with a total dislike of teenagers.

Mr. Kiersey started to chuckle.

"No," China added, frowning. "It couldn't be him."

"Why not?" Mr. Kiersey asked, obviously enjoying the game.

"Because he thinks all teenagers are dangerous. So he wouldn't trust an 18-year-old either." Then China slumped back in the chair. "I really can't work in the kitchen anymore?"

Mr. Kiersey shook his head.

China's eyes flew wide open. "That means I'm not useful to you anymore! I can't pay you for my room and board. I really do have to leave Camp Crazy Bear, don't I?" She clenched the armrests until her knuckles turned white.

A smile spread across Mr. Kiersey's face. "Do you want to stay?" he asked.

"Yes," she said softly. Then she sat up straight, her voice stronger. "That is, if you'll let me . . . I mean, that is, if you want me . . . I mean . . . I'll try to be useful."

Mr. Kiersey laughed. "China. It's okay. We want you to stay. We enjoy you."

"I'm not too much trouble?"

He stopped laughing and looked at her sideways. "Well, I wouldn't go so far as to say that."

China glanced down at her hands.

"You are—" He stopped and cleared his throat. "Actually you're really good for Deedee." He paused. "Even with all the trouble."

China licked her lips. "I'm sorry for all the trouble."

Mr. Kiersey laughed again. "I know you are. If you weren't remorseful, you'd be a different kind of person, and you wouldn't be living with us. You don't mean any harm. It just happens."

China's face brightened, and she looked him full in the face. "Thanks, Mr. Kiersey."

No one spoke for a few moments, then China said, "If that's all, I should let you get back to work." She started to stand.

"One more thing . . ." Mr. Kiersey said.

China sat down and waited.

"Are hugs allowed?"

China jumped from her chair and ran around the desk. Mr. Kiersey stood and held her like she'd seen him hold his own children many times. He let go and chucked her underneath her chin. "Magda said she'd whip you good if you didn't go see her a lot."

"Am I allowed in the kitchen?"

"Yes, but I have to find out what the law says about any restrictions. You might be able to help serve."

"But the campers do most of that."

"I know. But Magda doesn't want to lose you."

"She can't get rid of me."

Mr. Kiersey smiled. "That's what I told her." He ruffled her hair. "You'd better go find that daughter of mine before she bursts from curiosity."

China had half expected Deedee to fall into the office when she opened the door, but Deedee wasn't there. She wasn't outside the administration building either. She was probably still asleep.

Instead of going back to the Kiersey house, China trudged to the camp kitchen. She couldn't believe she wouldn't be working there anymore. After room and board came out of her paycheck, she really didn't earn that much, but she liked being with Magda. She adored singing and waltzing around the kitchen with Rick. She wouldn't miss the dirty dishes or the glop the high school kids liked to create with their leftovers. Too often it looked like someone had heaved into a dinner plate. She wouldn't miss that part at all.

The sun's rays baked the top of her head. She grabbed her hair into a ponytail, wishing she had something to hold it up off her hot, sticky neck. She tried walking closer to the shade cast by the trees, but the shadows weren't long enough yet.

This week's batch of high school kids screamed and shouted from the playing field. Little Bear Lake lay still without breeze or swimmers to ruffle the water's surface.

China walked up the hill to Eelapuash, the dining hall. She went around the back to the kitchen and slipped through the screen door.

Magda held the stainless Hobart bowl in her hands and dumped sticky dough onto the floured work table. She dipped her hands into the flour then pressed them into the dough.

China moved quietly to stand beside her. "Magda, why didn't you tell me?"

Magda sighed, wiping her hands on her apron. She missed a lot of the flour, which ended up on China as Magda cupped her cheeks. "Oh, China honey. I hoped the law wouldn't go through." She sighed again, dusting off China's face with her apron. "I didn't want to buy any trouble. I guess I'm superstitious in a way. If I don't talk about something ugly, it won't happen."

Magda was right. If China had known the law was out there, hanging over her head, her attitude would have been different. Her work would have suffered. She had been better off not knowing.

China moved about the kitchen, touching things as if to say good-bye to old friends. How could she get so attached in just a few weeks? *Memories,* she thought.

Memories give you an anchor to silly things and places.

"Just because you can't work here doesn't mean you can't come by and visit," Magda said. The words sounded more like a plea than a statement.

China plopped onto a stool and hung her head. "It won't be the same, Magda."

"Now, China honey. I don't want you missing out on all of God's wonderful opportunities because you're sitting here moping. Don't you know that He works through all things? He's got something else for you to do."

"I suppose," China replied, not really feeling it at all. "What if I won't like what He has for me to do?"

"You know I won't lie to you. That is possible. But it's only because He wants to teach you something good."

"Kinda like broccoli, huh, Magda? It's good for you, but it doesn't necessarily taste all that great." China looked full into Magda's face.

"Yes, ma'am. When the Bible says in Romans 8:28 that all things work together for good for them that love God, that word *good* doesn't necessarily mean *happy*. What's good for you and me is sometimes somethin' like broccoli. It ain't what we'd choose, but by George, it's good for us."

China tried to force a smile. She knew it came out looking oddly flat. "I know you're right, Magda. It just doesn't feel good right now."

"Of course not! Where in the Bible does it say you're going to feel good? It says it will *be* good. It *is* good. Not that it feels good." Magda's rolling pin flattened the ball of dough.

"You'd think with all my years in Guatemala I'd know that by now, Magda. But honestly, I've yet to see what's been good about my life."

Magda took out a round metal biscuit cutter and plunged it over and over into the dough. "There are many of God's lessons that take us years of schooling to learn. Don't beat yourself up. Just try to learn as best you can. He's patient."

China popped a piece of stray dough into her mouth. "Good thing He is, because I'm not."

The screen door opened at the far side of the kitchen. They heard Deedee's boots before they could see her.

"Hey, China! What gives?" Deedee called, as she rounded the corner. "Hi, Magda."

Deedee glared at China. "I've been dying to know what's going on. Dad wouldn't tell me. And here you are bugging Magda as if you don't see her enough already."

"That's going to change drastically," China said. As China filled Deedee in, Deedee's face took on a look of concern.

"Are you going to have to go live with Aunt Liddy now?" Deedee asked.

China shook her head and winked. "Not as long as I am good."

Deedee threw back her head, gesturing to the heavens. "She'll be gone by the end of the week if she lasts that long." She looked at China again. "How do you feel about all this?"

"Pretty crummy. I feel kind of useless."

"Well!" Magda said, clapping her hands together. "I can make you feel useful again!"

China threw Deedee a wild look. "Should I trust this woman?"

Deedee looked Magda up and down. While Magda pretended to primp, then tipped her chin up in a haughty look, Deedee said, "Hmmm, I think not."

Magda stuck out her bottom lip.

China crossed her arms and said, "Well, I suppose I could at least listen to your proposal, Magda."

Magda smiled and went back to her biscuits. "Actually, I'm glad you're both here. What I have to say is to both of you."

Deedee shrugged when China glanced at her.

Magda pretended to speak to herself. "Should I appeal to their miserly side? Or should I appeal to the part of them that would love to do anything for their dear old Magda?"

"Speak, woman!" China commanded. "Speak to both sides at once!"

Deedee turned to show Magda one cheek, then the other.

Magda turned to face them, excitement showing in

her eyes. "I've got this grand opportunity for the two of you to make a fair amount of money. And at the same time, you'll be helping out my cousin."

"I didn't know your cousin was anywhere around here," China said. It suddenly occurred to her that she hadn't ever thought of Magda as having family. Magda was just Magda.

"He just moved here. He's the new director of children's ministries." Magda glanced at the clock and jumped. She opened a large oven and shoved three trays of biscuits inside. She set the timer and returned to clump stray pieces of dough together and roll them out again.

Deedee's brows pulled together. "What happened to the Townsends?"

"You're out of touch, girl," Magda said. "They moved to Camp Kariwyo to be the executive directors there."

Deedee tilted her head and stared off into the distance. "How did I miss that?"

"Too much time with me," China sighed. "I'm just a bother."

Deedee whacked her friend playfully on the back of the head. "I don't think so."

Magda punched and rolled the dough. "Pete and Mary Macon."

"What?" China asked.

"Pete and Mary Macon. That's my cousin and his wife. They've got six adorable kids."

"Six!" Deedee clutched her throat. "If my mother gets any ideas from them . . ."

"Honey," Magda said through heavy-lidded eyes, "your mama has her own ideas."

"I don't want to think about it," Deedee said.

China jumped off her stool. "So how can we help your cousin? Do they need help unpacking? We can do that."

Deedee nodded. "Sure, anything to help would be fine with us."

China smiled, feeling generous. "Now that I don't have a job, it would be nice to do something for someone else."

Magda's smile grew wider. A chuckle bounced through her ample body. "You're really willing to help?" she asked.

The girls nodded.

"They need a baby-sitter."

Deedee's eyes widened.

China gulped and forced a smile. "Sure . . . okay. When?"

"This weekend."

"Yes, but which day?" Deedee asked.

"They have to go to a seminar, since they're new to camping," Magda told them. "The only time it's offered is this weekend. I would baby-sit, but I have to work."

"But which day?" Deedee said, panic rising in her voice.

"The whole weekend."

Deedee's voice came out in a squeak. "Six kids? The whole weekend?"

"How much are they paying?" China asked.

Deedee stared at China. "As if that would make a difference."

"It might," China said and turned to Magda. "How much?"

"I believe Administration is going to help pay for the sitter."

"That doesn't answer my question."

"Really," Magda said, "when you think about the hours involved, you won't make that much."

Deedee poked China. "She's giving us the run-around."

China smiled and put her hands on her hips. "How much?"

"One hundred dollars."

The girls gasped.

"That's less than $3 an hour for 36 hours," Magda warned them.

"We'll do it!" China said. She looked at Deedee's panic-stricken face. "It can't be that hard, Deeds."

Magda clapped her hands together, and bits of dough and flour burst forth in a cloud. "My, that's fine! I told the Macons you were the two sweetest girls anyone could ever meet."

Deedee just stared at them both.

CHAPTER TWO

"**W**HAT CAME OVER YOU?" Deedee almost shrieked the words at China. "Six kids for a whole weekend? Are you out of your mind?"

"How bad could it be?" China asked. "It's only Friday night to Sunday breakfast. We can do that."

Deedee's deep red curls whipped the air as she shook her head. "You're out of your mind, China. Completely. Totally."

"Think about it! That's $50 each. Little kids aren't all that hard to deal with. I've always found baby-sitting to be boring more than anything else. So we'll be bored for a whole weekend. Big deal. At least we're helping Magda. . . . I feel like I owe her so much."

"Well, I don't owe her anything," Deedee said.

"She's always been good to you."

Deedee sighed. "I know. I'm sorry. I just hate being around little kids. They make me crazy."

"But it will be so different from taking care of your sisters and brothers. Besides, they're paying an awful lot of money," China reminded her. "Your mom said it was okay—and a great idea."

"She would," Deedee grumped. "She's always trying to get me to be around kids. Probably so I'll be more helpful at home." She kicked a small rock and watched it tumble away. She kicked another even harder.

"If you're so upset, let's tell Magda it won't work out."

Deedee shook her head. "It's the right thing to do. I'll get over my mood. Leave me alone for a while."

─೫─

By the next morning, Deedee had reconciled with the whole idea. The hot, still air inside the cabin drove the girls to the shady deck with beading glasses of iced tea. China rolled the glass across her forehead.

Deedee plopped onto a plastic chair and used her feet to push off her hiking boots. She slipped off her socks with her big toe and rested her heels inside the boots to avoid deck splinters.

China lay on the deck in the shade, her tawny hair dripping through the slats to the cool darkness below. "I wish I could fit under there," she said.

"I'll show you the crawl space," Deedee said. "You can join the bugs and garbage the boys have dropped down there."

"You're so sweet, Deedee dear. I can't wait to see how you treat Magda's family."

"You know," Deedee said, "maybe this won't be so bad. We can make this a kind of mini-Tribal Village experience. Make crafts, go on a nature walk . . ."

"Great idea. We could give them swimming lessons." China snapped her fingers. "We could surprise the parents by helping the kids unpack their rooms."

"It's going to be okay," Deedee said, catching a bit of China's energy. "It won't necessarily be fun, but we can do this."

"Trust me," China said, smiling. "We can make anything fun."

Deedee cupped her hands over her ears and squished her eyes shut. "Don't say it!"

China pried Deedee's hands off her ears. "Trust me," she whispered. "Trust me," she said in a husky voice. "TRUST ME!" China laughed and looked at a scowling Deedee. "How can a good Christian girl like you be superstitious?" she asked.

Deedee shook her head. "I'm not superstitious, but you have this knack . . ."

"Isn't that what superstition is? Someone notices a word or an act that seems to be followed by disaster. . . ."

"Fine. I'm superstitious when it comes to you."

China laughed.

Inside the house, the phone rang. The girls ignored it, trying not to move in the oppressive heat.

"Maybe we should go swimming," Deedee said.

"Good idea. But I'm too hot to move."

Ring-g-g-g.

Mrs. Kiersey's voice floated through the screen

door. "Hello? Yes, they're here. Just a minute."

Deedee moved slowly to unstick her skin from the vinyl and nudged China with her foot. "Phone," she said.

"Not interested."

Mrs. Kiersey looked through the screen. "It's Kemper. He says it's urgent he speaks to both of you."

"With Kemper, everything is urgent," Deedee said. "I think it's part of the genetic makeup of a high school camp director. Come on, China, I can't face him alone."

"Tell him we're busy," China said. "We can't try out whatever torture device he's come up with this time."

Deedee tugged on China's slack arm. "You tell him better than I do. I'm a pushover."

"True." China groaned as she got to her feet. She tip-toed carefully across the deck, hoping to avoid splinters.

Deedee picked up the receiver and held it so they both could hear. "Hi, Kemp!"

"I've got an incredibly wonderful plan for you two!" Kemper's voice boomed so loud that both girls jerked their heads away from the receiver. "Hey. This is the wildest. This is the greatest. And I think . . . no, I *know* you girls will go crazy when I tell you this plan."

China rolled her eyes at Deedee.

"I'm sure we will," Deedee said into the phone. She held it away from her ear before Kemper started to talk again.

"I guess some wealthy donor to Camp Crazy Bear has decided to take a bunch of kids on his houseboat for four days," he said. "He's got a ski boat, jet skis . . . you know, the basic life of poverty. His kids are grown and gone, and he's imported some teens on a foreign-exchange program from Europe. He'd like some American teens to join the fun."

China's heart skipped a beat. *Houseboating? Skiing?* "Jet skis?" she said aloud.

"How about it? You girls care to host some kids from Europe?"

China nodded at Deedee. Deedee practically screamed into the phone. "Are you kidding? We'd love to? When is it?"

Kemper cleared his throat. "Uh, well, that's the only problem."

"What, Kemper?" Deedee asked.

China bit her bottom lip, and without thinking, she crossed her fingers.

"This is kind of late notice. You'd need to go this Thursday."

"As in day after tomorrow?" Deedee asked.

China's heart sank.

"Yeah. You'd come back late Sunday night."

"I'll call you back," Deedee said, and hung up the phone.

"Tell me this isn't happening," China said, sliding down the wall until she sat on the floor.

Deedee dropped to the floor beside China and put her head in her hands. "Why? Why? Why?" she repeated.

"Gee," China said, "which would you rather do? Go houseboating and skiing, or watch six kids? My, oh my. I don't think I can decide."

The girls silently stared at the floor.

Deedee picked at some lint and rolled it into a ball, then stretched it out as far as it would go. "Maybe we can call Magda and tell her we can't do it after all. Mom won't let us. Or we're getting sick. Or we're needed somewhere else."

China searched Deedee's face. "We're terrible liars."

Deedee went back to stretching lint.

China continued to look at Deedee. "How could we let Magda down?" she asked. "I can't lie to Magda."

"Then let's tell her the truth."

China gave Deedee a flat smile and said, "You tell her. I'll wait outside to call 911."

"Okay, then, Miss 'Trust Me,' you figure out a way for us to go."

China stared at the carpet until it became a blur. She let her thoughts spin and swirl. She thought of a million lies, and all the reasons why she and Deedee should go on the houseboat trip rather than baby-sit. After all, they were just kids, and it was their time in life to have fun. They had agreed to help only because of Magda. Certainly there were many other people who would be willing to make that kind of money watching kids.

Someone who actually liked kids. A professional, perhaps. Besides, the Macons, having just moved to Crazy Bear, probably shouldn't leave their poor children, anyway. It might scar their precious psyches for life.

China didn't know how long she had been lost in thought. When she looked up, Deedee was pouring more iced tea into her glass.

"Let's just call Magda and tell her we'll help her find someone else," China said. "It shouldn't be that hard. And then we can go on the houseboat trip with a clear conscience."

Deedee placed the phone in China's lap. "Fine with me. You call her."

China dialed the extension for Eelapuash. "Hi, Magda. I wanted to talk to you about this weekend."

"The Macons are looking forward to it, China honey. They want their children to meet the local families. And this will be a great way to do it. Besides, it means so much to me. I know there are other things you girls could be doing. It's a nice sacrifice."

China dropped her head and looked sideways at Deedee. She mouthed, "I can't do this."

Deedee's face contorted as she whispered instructions. "Do it! Talk to her."

"I can't," China mouthed again.

"You chicken."

"China honey?" Magda's voice came over the phone. "What did you want to talk to me about?"

"You know, Magda," China said brightly, "there are other things Deedee and I could be doing. And that's what I was calling about. Something has come up. Kemper has asked us to help host some kids from Europe on a little weekend outing. So we're very sorry, but we can't baby-sit for you."

A stony silence filled the next several seconds.

"I'm sure it would be easy to find someone else to baby-sit these fine children," China continued.

Deedee gave her a big smile and a thumbs-up. China wished she could see Magda's face. She wondered if Magda was disappointed. But she was easygoing and understanding. Didn't Magda always say that China and Deedee were sweet? She'd be delighted to see them go have fun.

After a long pause, Magda spoke. "Do you have more to say?"

China thought her voice sounded funny. "Yes," she answered. "We can help you find an alternate sitter."

"I don't think so." Magda's voice definitely sounded stilted now, and there was something else. "You girls made a promise, and I expect you to keep it." She hung up the phone.

China stared at the phone receiver, not believing that Magda would actually hang up on her.

"What did she say?" Deedee asked, bouncing up and down.

"She hung up on me," China said.

Deedee stopped bouncing. "Oh."

"She sounded like Aunt Liddy—on PMS."

Deedee grimaced. "Ohhh. That's bad."

"She said we made a promise, and she expects us to keep it."

Mrs. Kiersey walked in, dust rag in hand, and dangled it from her fingers. "Which of you would like to dust?"

Two limp arms rose halfheartedly in the air.

Mrs. Kiersey sat on the floor between them. "Why so glum? What kind of terrible news did Kemper give you?"

"It wasn't terrible news," Deedee said.

"It was a fabulous, wonderful, exciting opportunity," China said.

"It doesn't seem too wonderful by the looks on your faces," Mrs. Kiersey said. Then she remained silent, waiting for one of the girls to speak.

Deedee finally said, "Kemper invited us to go on a houseboat-skiing trip with some kids visiting from Europe."

Mrs. Kiersey sat up straighter. "Well, that does sound wonderful. So what's the problem? I'm sure if we know who's in charge, we can arrange for you two to go."

China drew patterns in the rug. "That's not the problem. We promised to baby-sit for the Macons the same weekend." She looked up at Mrs. Kiersey. "I guess Magda talked to you before she asked us."

Mrs. Kiersey nodded. "She did. That's this weekend, correct?"

Both girls nodded.

"And Kemper's trip is also this weekend?"

"Why else would we feel so lousy?" Deedee said. "Can't we get out of baby-sitting, Mom? Can you help us figure out a way so we can go on the houseboat? This would be my first time."

"Mine, too," China said. "And I've never been water-skiing either."

Hope began to build inside China. Moms were good at helping kids out of tough spots.

"It does sound like a lot of fun," Mrs. Kiersey said, looking at Deedee. "I suppose it is more enticing than baby-sitting six kids."

China sat up straighter, afraid to say anything. She watched Deedee nod yes emphatically.

Mrs. Kiersey pressed her lips together. "Sometimes I don't like my job as mother," she admitted.

Yeah, China agreed silently, *it's tough to have to do the dirty work for your timid kids sometimes.*

Mrs. Kiersey put her hand on Deedee's arm. "And this is certainly one of those times. It's my role to teach you and guide you. And sometimes I have to say things you don't want to hear."

Well, okay, China thought, *you tell us how to back out, and we'll do the dirty work. I guess it's time we grow up. Not that I don't want to grow up. There are just some parts of life I'd rather leave to those who've done it before.*

Mrs. Kiersey looked at her daughter. "You're going to roll your eyes at this one. It's mother lecture time."

Sure enough, Deedee rolled her eyes, then blushed at getting caught.

Mrs. Kiersey spoke in a low tone. "The Bible says we must abide by our commitments. Our yes must be yes, and our no must be no."

China felt hope slip away.

"If you want to do what is right, you must be true to your commitment to Magda and the Macons."

Had she been listening on the extension? China wondered.

"But Mom," Deedee protested, "we didn't know about the houseboat trip when we said yes. We didn't have all the information to make a wise decision."

Mrs. Kiersey nodded her agreement. "Our decisions are made with whatever information we have at the moment. If you had suspicions that something else would come up later, you could have said no or waited to give an answer." Mrs. Kiersey took Deedee's hands in her own. "Sweetheart, living with the consequences of the choices you make is one of the most difficult lessons you will ever learn. The right thing to do here is to honor your commitment—stand by the choice you made."

China wanted to stick out her tongue. Doing right could be such a pain. Hey, weren't women supposed to change their minds all the time?

"You girls are old enough now that I'm not going to tell you what to do. The choice is yours."

"What if we choose to go on the ski trip?" Deedee asked.

Mrs. Kiersey shrugged. "Look at it from the perspective of others around the camp. Would they trust you the next time to complete a task you started? Would Magda's relationship with you change?" Mrs. Kiersey wrapped a red Deedee curl around her finger. "I'll leave you with this thought: If God's way of living life were easy, you'd have the whole world following it. Instead, God's way is incredibly difficult. And I'm one who wishes it wasn't."

China felt odd—like she'd intruded into something personal.

Mrs. Kiersey ripped the dust rag in two and handed half to each girl. "It seems to me that you could think about your decision while you dust. Thanks for helping." She kissed each girl on top of the head and then stood up and left the room.

CHAPTER THREE

THE DUST TICKLED CHINA'S NOSE and made her sneeze. She hated dusting but couldn't very well tell Mrs. Kiersey no. If she were at home, she would have begged for a different chore. Instead, she shoved a wad of tissue into the pocket of her cutoff jeans and pulled one out every so often as she wiped dust and sneezed all around the living room. Deedee finally stopped saying "Bless you."

"There's got to be a way we can go on the house-boat trip," Deedee said, as she crawled under the dining room table to dust the chair rungs. "Isn't there some way to do it so we won't hurt Magda's feelings?"

China attacked the window ledges and picture frames with her dust rag. "It's not fair" was all she said.

"Have you ever been on a houseboat?" Deedee asked.

"No, but I've always wanted to."

"Me, too."

China blew her nose again. "Maybe there's still a way we can do this," she said.

"You've got the brain that thinks up things," Deedee said. "Put it to work!"

They finished dusting the living room in silence to let China brainstorm. *Music would help,* she thought. Music would soothe and distract her so that her mind could whirl on its own. Usually she tried in vain to get her mind off the many tangents it could go on. But for some reason, the whirling had stopped.

China moved through the hallway, dusting endless family photographs lining the walls. She tried to jump-start her brain with visions of whales walking through camp on tiptoe. She couldn't even picture herself standing on the shores of a lake. It felt like someone had drained her brain and left empty air behind.

Deedee did a poor job of pretending not to look at China. After every few swipes of the dust cloth, she'd look up.

"Quit it!" China finally said.

"I was hoping to see if you got any great ideas."

"You can't see through my skull!"

"No, but I thought maybe a great idea would show on your face."

"Leave me alone."

China felt crabby through and through. This was probably her only chance of ever going on a house-boat, and she couldn't think of one way to get out of baby-sitting for Magda's cousin.

Deedee sat on the top stair and dropped the dust rag between her feet. China sat beside her, leaning against the wall.

"So, what did you come up with?" Deedee asked.

China made a zero with her thumb and fingers. "Nada."

Deedee stared at her bare feet. "We could tell Magda the truth. We could be jerks and just not go."

"Would we have any fun on the houseboat?"

China hated herself for saying that, but she knew it was true. All weekend they would have guilt pangs.

"We'd have lots of fun and you know it," Deedee snapped. "We'd just feel terrible in between having fun."

China put her chin on her knees. "It's a lousy thing to know what's right and have to do it."

"So we're stuck, aren't we?"

China sighed. "We might as well make the best of it."

"Mom always says God rewards obedience," Deedee said. "Maybe if we obey, He'll do something nice for us."

"The nicest thing He could do would be to let us go on the trip. The problem is, He can be two places at once, but we can't," China said glumly. "I want to be on that houseboat. And I have no clue how to stick by our original choice to baby-sit and be on the houseboat, too."

"I'm surprised you're not even trying," Deedee said.

China rested her head on Deedee's back. "Should we really try?" China asked.

Deedee tried to shake her head with her hair pinned beneath China's head. "No," she whispered instead.

"You know, Deedee, I'd really like to pound my head against the wall and repeat 'stupid, stupid, stupid' so I don't make rash choices in the future."

"Fat chance that would do any good."

China thumped Deedee lightly on the head. "Nice to have a friend who has faith in me."

"Anytime, China dear, anytime."

China closed her eyes and said softly, "God, this is really stupid. I think it's mean that You let us know about the houseboat after we said yes to baby-sitting. You could have let us know before. Since You didn't, we'll just have to live with it. To be incredibly honest, we're not happy about sticking with our original choice. I hope it's okay with You that we will follow through with the commitment, even though we'd rather do something else." China sighed heavily.

"Amen," Deedee added. "You know, China, sometimes I wonder what God thinks of your prayers."

"If He needs me to talk to Him in a special way, then I'm in big trouble," China said. "I suppose it's not even His fault that we didn't hear about the houseboat trip first. But it would be so much nicer to get mad at somebody else for my stupid choices than to blame myself."

"I hate growing up," Deedee said, and slowly got to her feet. "We might as well get to work trying to figure out what we're going to do to keep six kids happy for a day and a half."

"Television," China said. "We'll watch lots and lots of TV. Maybe we can even watch 'Family Squabbles.' "

China called Eelapuash for the second time. "I'm sorry, Magda," she forced herself to say. "We'll be there whenever you say."

Magda sighed. "Seven-thirty, Friday night," she said. Then her voice took on the softness China knew so well. "Thank you, China honey. Good-bye." The phone clicked gently into a dial tone.

China hung up feeling like one of the crummiest people ever to walk the earth.

*

China felt cranky. No matter how hard she tried, she couldn't seem to find anything good in sticking with the choice she had made. Sure it was the right thing to do. Somehow that knowledge didn't make her feel any better. Every time she walked out the front door into the solid heat, she could imagine the cool spray on her as she water-skied. Every time she went to bed, her bed was too stable—it didn't rock gently on a cushion of water.

China felt bad that she didn't even want to talk to Deedee. She supposed it didn't really matter, since Deedee was off in her own little world. She, too, looked sad and disappointed.

Mr. Kiersey tried to tease the girls at dinner time. China forced a smile that came out crooked and insincere. She saw a look pass between Mrs. Kiersey and Mr. Kiersey. Then he raised his eyebrows, shrugged, and turned his teasing to Joseph and Adam.

Friday dawned brighter and hotter than any day preceding it. China wished she could sleep the day away so she wouldn't have to remember the trip she was missing. Her mind, not in sync with her emotions, woke her brightly. Deedee slumbered on, breathing heavily in the bed above her.

China lay on her sleeping bag on the floor, her hands behind her head, and stared at the ceiling. She wanted to pray, but she was mad at God. She knew He could have arranged circumstances differently. But He hadn't. She knew He had the power to have the parents of the six-pack change their minds and not go to their seminar. But He didn't. Did God care that they would miss the ski trip? China tried to convince herself there must be something terrible going to happen on the ski trip that they were being saved from. But deep down inside, she knew that as long as she'd known God, He often didn't make sense.

China willed herself not to talk to a God who didn't want the most fun thing for her, or give her what she figured was the best thing for her. Only God knew why. And He wasn't sharing any of His information.

Why had she given her life to such a God in the first

place? Why had she decided that she would receive His gift of erasing her stupid actions as if they had never existed? Right now, she wished He would do the forgiveness thing and still give her all the fun and good things in life.

When she'd said yes to God, she really wanted His guidance and for Him to change her into the best China Jasmine Tate she could be. She never knew it would be so hard.

Sometimes I really don't like You, God. China sighed. She couldn't honestly feel that way for long. After all, when she had been a counselor at the kids' camp and Heather got stranded on the mountain, God had been the one nudging China to rescue her . . . even though Heather didn't deserve it. And although that didn't feel very good at first, the result had been something China would never have expected.

She sighed again. *Okay, God. Have it Your way.*

Suddenly, she felt an odd peace. She still wanted desperately to go water-skiing. She still didn't like it that God demanded she do what went against her own desires. But a thread of peace looped around through all her negative feelings. Somehow it seemed okay that she really wasn't delighted about the situation. She didn't have to be.

China rolled over and reached underneath Deedee's bed for a small box. Inside were a writing pad with Tweety Bird in the bottom corner, matching envelopes, and calligraphy pens. She stuffed her pillow underneath her stomach, chose a lavender pen, and began to draw curlicues around the border. Why was it so easy to write 10-page letters to friends and so difficult to think of anything to say to her mother?

She wrote the first words, hoping that would stimulate more.

Dear Mom,

China paused, chewing on the end of her pen.

The mosquitoes are getting bigger as the summer gets hotter. I think one day they'll carry off a small kid or something.

Well, China said to herself, *that was a pretty dumb thing to write. At least it keeps the paper from being too blank.* She continued writing:

How is everybody? We're all fine. Anna's head is healing nicely. She's talking again, but still only one word at a time. I wish you could meet this family. I think you'd really like them. Especially Mrs. Kiersey. Dad and Mr. Kiersey could trade stupid jokes.

Then China felt bad about what she'd written. After all the struggles she'd had with her parents, here she was saying nice things about another family. It wasn't that she ever really meant any of the mean things she had said to her parents. She was only feeling weird inside and didn't know how to deal with the stuff she thought was making her crazy.

China smiled and wrote,

They are a lot like you.

There. That ought to make things better.

Bologna is fine. He is really Rick's dog now. He still likes us, but he wags mostly for Rick. That's okay. Rick needed Bologna and Bologna needed Rick.

China tried to draw a little dog, but it came out looking like a purple blob with sticks poking out of the bottom.

Deedee and I are going to baby-sit six kids this weekend. It's really only for one full day. This ought to be an adventure.

China closed the letter with "hugs and kisses." She folded up the pages and put them in the envelope. She really missed her family. She was beginning to think it wasn't so bad being a missionary kid after all. Being an MK gave her the opportunity to experience life and other people and cultures. She realized she *loved* that about being an MK.

Hopefully, this weekend she'd see something equally good come out of sticking with her commitments. She sure didn't see it now.

CHAPTER FOUR

AT BREAKFAST, ANNA SAT IN HER HIGH CHAIR, stuffing Cheerios into her mouth by the handful. She giggled when China walked into the room. She raised her hands into the air and opened them. A shower of Cheerios rained down, and she laughed some more.

"You silly girl," China said, kissing the top of her head. Several Cheerios stuck to Anna's damp hands. China took Anna's wrist and ate a couple from her hands. "Yummy!" she said.

Anna's baby laugh cackled.

China was relieved that Anna seemed to be returning to normal after the bear attack at the beginning of summer. Of course, she couldn't talk much yet, but she looked happy, and the scars were healing.

"I'm eating eggs," Eve said. "I'm bigger than Anna and I like eggs better and I don't make a mess out of Cheerios like Anna does and I already had one toast with cinnamon and now I'm having toast with straw-berry jam. What are you going to have?"

"What do you think I should have?" China asked her.

"I thought you didn't like breakfast and that you like Lucky Charms and I like those, too, but Mommy says we don't have any more because you and Deedee eat them for snacks when you really should only eat them for breakfast, so there aren't any more for you to have so you have to have Cheerios or eggs or oatmeal. I think Mommy made lots of eggs, but Joseph didn't want any, so now there are lots left because Daddy had to leave for work and he didn't eat any either."

China sat at her usual place. "Eggs will be fine then."

"They might be kind of cold, but we can put them in the microwave if you like them hot, but then they might get too hot and you'd have to wait anyway."

"I'm sure they'll be fine." China looked around the table. Joseph held a small matchbox car and some kind of action figure that he marched through the utensils and cups. He made no sounds, but China could see the intensity of imagination in his face.

Adam scowled at his eggs. China wondered who or what he was angry at until she saw him glaring on occasion at his mother, his own toys on the telephone table.

Each of these kids has some kind of fun and wonderful quality about them. I bet the kids we baby-sit will be special, too. China rolled her eyes at herself. *Gross! I'm getting cheesy.*

Deedee must have accepted their weekend plans.

She appeared, looking damp and peaceful, long after the breakfast mess had been cleaned up and the kids had gone their separate ways to play. Sitting at the dining table, she blotted her wet hair with a giant towel. "Nine more hours," she said.

China nodded.

"What do you want to do?"

"Get cooled off."

"Creek, lake, or pool?"

"Creek," China said. "It may be the only solitude we have for hours."

"It's going to be okay, isn't it?" Deedee asked.

"Yeah. . . . It might even be fun."

Deedee shook her head gently. "We folks who try to look on the good side of things can be awfully disgusting."

China smiled. "I don't want to think about it. I want to play my day in denial."

Deedee laughed. "It's a deal."

⤳

"Why do hot days always go slower than cold ones?" Deedee asked, as they relaxed in the cool of their shady, bush-lined hideaway near the creek.

Goose bumps prickled China's skin. Usually she hated them. In the intense heat of this day, she rather enjoyed them. "Maybe because everyone is moving in slow motion."

"We should go get ready," Deedee said, looking at

her black Swatch. "Only two more hours. Dinner in one hour."

"After I dry off I want to do one more dunk in the creek."

"You've said that the last three dunks."

China's mouth formed an evil grin. "I know."

Deedee pretended to smack her. "You've had your last dunk."

"Thank you, Mother Doughnut."

"*China!*" Deedee moaned loudly in mock exasperation. "I think I'm going to have a tougher time with you than with the kids."

When the girls reached the Kiersey cabin, Mrs. Kiersey met them with a message that they weren't needed until 8:00.

"A stay of execution," China muttered.

"Do you have a last request?" Mrs. Kiersey asked solemnly.

"Something cold," China replied.

Mrs. Kiersey grinned. "I just bought Eskimo Pies. How 'bout one after dinner?"

"Deal!" China said.

The girls spent the next hour gathering construction paper, crayons, glue, paints, and other doodads for entertaining the kids. They packed all the goodies in one bag and a change of clothes in another. Mrs. Kiersey sent them off with Eskimo Pies, and Mr. Kiersey accompanied them with a flashlight. It wasn't quite dark yet, but just in case they hit a dense spot in the forest, he liked to be prepared.

"Daddy," Deedee protested. "I think we can find the way."

"What if the Abdominal Forest Guy is out here?" he asked, looking around in an exaggerated effort.

"D-a-d-d-y," Deedee moaned. "We're not little kids. Besides, it's the Abominable Snowman."

"To be honest—" Mr. Kiersey looked back at the house and lowered his voice "—I want a walk without little kids for a change, and this is a good excuse."

Deedee looked at her dad out of the corner of her eye, not sure if she believed him or not.

China recognized the sheepish look on his face. "You can't come unless you have your own Eskimo Pie," she told him, as if she were someone in authority. "I won't have you mooching bites off mine."

Mr. Kiersey dashed back into the house.

"China!" Deedee said. "Whose side are you on, anyway?"

"It won't kill us," China said.

Mr. Kiersey reappeared, ripping the foil off the ice cream bar.

They moved westward through the forest, making their own path as they went. "The Macons don't have their phone hooked up yet," Mr. Kiersey said. "The phone company around here is slower than snot."

China's eyebrows shot up, and she tried to hide her smile.

"It's due to be hooked up next week. In the valley, all they have to do is flip a switch. We're not there yet."

"Who would we call, anyway?" Deedee asked. "We'll have our hands full as it is."

Deedee's father gave her a knowing look and said, "If you have an emergency, you'll have to come all the way home. We're the closest cabin. The Admin building may be a little closer, but . . . well, if something happens, you can decide which place to go to."

"I doubt anything bad's going to happen," China said, trying to reassure him.

Deedee shot her a look that would have severely wilted a more tender soul. China flashed her a fake smile in return.

"No one really knows much about this family," Mr. Kiersey said. "I was quite impressed with Pete Macon in the three interviews we had. And of course, Magda can give nothing but glowing reports about all of them." Mr. Kiersey stuck the damp ice cream stick into his shirt pocket.

"Dad, we can do this," Deedee said, obviously offended.

"I just wanted to give you some information ahead of time," he said defensively. "To prepare you. . . ."

Silence tore the friendliness between them. Neither attempted to repair it. Suddenly the forest seemed thick and gloomy rather than beautiful in the golden light of dusk. They walked the remaining distance without a word.

China tried to think of something clever to say to make everyone laugh and relax. But her stomach clenched on itself. Six kids? What had she been thinking? *Fifty dollars,* she reminded herself in a vain attempt to soothe her jitters.

Moments later, a spatter of warm lights beckoned them through the trees. Deedee reached over and linked pinkies with China for a quick moment.

China looked at her and smiled. "It's going to be okay," she said. "We might even have fun."

At that, Deedee put her head back and laughed. "Dad, are you coming back to pick up the remains?"

"No," Mr. Kiersey said casually. "I'll let someone else bury 'em."

Deedee slugged her father. "Thanks a lot."

"You're welcome a lot." He paused at the edge of the clearing. "Do you want me to come in?"

Deedee looked from China to the house and back to her father. "I think we're okay, Dad."

Mr. Kiersey looked disappointed.

"I didn't mean . . ." Deedee said, her voice filled with frustration.

Mr. Kiersey smiled slightly. "I know. You're just growing up, that's all."

"Oh, gag," Deedee said. She gave him a playful

shove. "Now go on before I get a sugar high from being around you."

He moved away a few steps, then stopped to watch the girls walk toward the house.

"It's actually kind of cute," China said, looking over her shoulder at the doting parent.

"You can say that because he's not your father," Deedee said, her steps quickening.

"True." China figured she'd be mortified if her father presented her to a baby-sitting job as though she were a child.

China hoisted her duffel bag over her shoulder and walked a little faster toward the cabin. In Crazy Bear-style, the two-story cabin sat in a cozy circle of protective trees. It seemed to China that every light must be on in the house. Each window stood in bright contrast to the dark, unfinished wood exterior. A large picture window let the girls see piles of boxes in the main room. Other windows showed off the kitchen and another large room. Upstairs, lights showed all the way around the top floor like candles on a Swedish girl's Santa Lucia crown. It made China think about Christmas and Pepper Kakor cookies, meatballs and pickled herring. A burst of homesickness hit her, then disappeared in a flash.

"Pretty, isn't it?" Deedee said. "Very homey."

"Just like your house."

Deedee put on her air of authority and knocked on

the door. A huge man with black hair tightly curled on his head opened the door with such force that China wondered how long the hinges would last. His pale-blue, short-sleeved dress shirt stretched against the buttons on his ample chest and stomach. He looked solid—like a stone wall. Perspiration marks made dark circles underneath his arms. He shoved a stray piece of shirttail into black polyester slacks.

"Can I help you?" he boomed.

Two excited dogs wiggled past him, swamping the girls with fast-acting tongues and wild sniffing. Their tails wagged so fast and hard that their hind ends wiggled, too.

"Jerome! Corky!" Mr. Macon shouted. "These girls are not Popsicles." The dogs paid no attention to him.

With a voice like that, China thought, *they're probably deaf.*

"It's okay," China said to Mr. Macon, as she dropped to her knees. "I love dogs. Don't I, fellas?" China rubbed and scratched behind the dogs' ears.

Deedee didn't seem daunted at all by this bigger-than-huge adult. "Hi," she said, sticking out her right hand. "I'm Deedee, and this is China."

"I'm Pete Macon," he said, his deep bass voice sounding like thunder as he shook her hand with gusto. "Come on in!" He opened the door wider, his massive body blocking most of their view of the living room.

A tall, large-boned woman strode into the room, a tiger-striped cat at her heels. A lutino cockatiel perched on her shoulder, preening its yellow feathers. The woman wore a shirtwaist dress that looked as though she'd probably gained a few pounds since she bought it.

China shrank back, expecting Mrs. Macon's voice to be like her husband's. Instead, a tinny-tiny voice contrasted with her sturdy looks.

"Welcome, girls," she said. "We're so pleased you would be willing to baby-sit our children. It's important we attend this seminar—it's only offered once a year—and we really thought we'd have to begin this new job without it. We sure appreciate your willingness." Her head dropped slightly to the right, as if putting a period on the sentence.

"We're delighted to be able to help," Deedee said.

China always let Deedee do the talking when it came to dealing with adults; such conversation came naturally to her. China, on the other hand, always fell into being herself—which didn't always go over well if the person didn't know her.

As Deedee and Mrs. Macon exchanged pleasantries, China looked around the room. The stacked boxes they'd seen from outside were actually in the corners of the room. Two sofas faced the river stone fireplace blackened with many previous fires. Old bedspreads covered the sofas—the kind that her mom hated taking naps on because they left their scrolled designs pressed into her cheek. One bedspread was green, the other blue. A wooden rocking chair sat off to one side. One of the rockers bore splintered chew marks. China sure hoped it was a four-legged youngster who made the marks.

Mrs. Macon, who insisted on being called Mary, moved toward the next room to give the girls a tour. A pocked trestle dining table dominated the corner room. Mismatched chairs stood around the table.

"I'm sorry we don't have curtains," Mary said. "We haven't had time to finish unpacking or decorate."

"That doesn't matter," Deedee said. "Out here you aren't on any well-used trail, so it's unlikely you have to worry about people looking in."

Mary stood at the picture window. "We only have animals to worry about," she said. "And we do like animals."

"So do we," Deedee said. "What kinds of animals do you have?"

China thought it was a dumb question, considering they'd probably already met all the family pets.

"You haven't met our fish and a housebroken bunny named Amelia. She's shy, but very sweet. She always comes out when the kids play."

A plus mark for the kids, China thought. *If the animals aren't afraid, they can't be too bad.*

Mary gestured toward the cockatiel on her shoulder. "Romeo here is a sweet bird. He's allowed to roam free during the day. Out there," she said, pointing near a metal storage shed, "is our pond. That's one of the reasons why we bought this house. We have frogs, turtles, and ducks. We only have one cat right now, but that's unusual."

"I do hope you left feeding instructions," Deedee said.

"The boys will feed the ducks in the morning. I'd like Emily to feed the dogs. If you wouldn't mind feeding the fish, the rabbit, the bird, and the cat, I'd appreciate it. All the instructions are right here on the kitchen counter with the phone number where we will be staying."

The kitchen was typical, but as Mary showed them the childproof latch on the knife drawer, China wanted to ask if she was sure it was okay for them to use sharp knives. After all, they were hormone-crazed teenagers.

"I'm really anxious to meet the children," Deedee said. "I haven't heard a peep from them."

Mary smiled. "They're in bed reading books until they could meet you." Her smile grew wider. "You're quite fortunate to be able to spend the weekend with them. They're such wonderful little people!"

"I'm sure they are," Deedee said, echoing Mary's reassuring tone.

China, on the other hand, felt sick to her stomach. Something wasn't right. And she was afraid they'd find out soon enough what her intuition was trying to tell her.

CHAPTER FIVE

CHINA AND DEEDEE FOLLOWED MARY up the narrow staircase, dodging the dogs, who chased the cat between and around their legs.

At the top, Mary put one finger to her lips and held out her hand to stop them.

Peering around her, they saw two large boogie men moving stealthily down the hallway away from them. The "monsters" wore brown bear heads. A lion's coat with cut-outs for the eyes covered the middle. Black snakeskin covered skinny legs that looked way too small for the height of the creatures. The creatures crept down the hall, heading for the last door on the right.

Mary stopped, her hands on her hips, and waited patiently. China supposed she waited for them to turn around.

One of the boogie men peered inside the room. Without looking back, he motioned for the other to follow.

Mary's head wagged back and forth. China recognized the motherly shake of the head. She'd seen her own mother do it many times. Mary looked back at the girls, motioned for them to follow her, then tiptoed down the hall. A foot from the last door, she motioned for the girls to flatten themselves against the wall, then gave them a conspiratorial smile and waited.

The two boogie men spoke in muffled tones to each other. "Where'd they go?" one asked.

The second one shrugged. "They should be here."

"Mom said we had to get in bed."

"Let's go take our stuff off and tell on them."

China and Deedee followed Mary's example by stepping out from the wall, crossing their arms, and standing with feet wide apart, a stern expression on their faces.

The boogie men rounded the corner, no longer trying to be slow or quiet. In their intense concentration to tattle on their sisters, they paid no attention to where they were going. As they slammed into a human wall, the boogie men screamed and fell back, landing on their backsides. Bearskin headdresses came off identical brown heads, revealing identical freckled faces, small perfect noses, long eyelashes, and ears that stuck straight out from their heads.

The boy in front of China stuck his finger in his ear.

The other boy looked at his mother and started talking fast. "You said we had to get in bed and so we went to make sure the girls were in bed and they weren't and so we were just coming to get you." His impish smile ended the sentence.

Mary shook her head again. China wondered if she did it to clear the cobwebs from her brain in order to know how to respond to something so ridiculous. Or did she count to 10 to keep from screaming at them?

Whatever it was, she said, "So why didn't I get the news?"

"What news?" both boys asked.

"That Daddy had left the country and left you two in charge?"

"Oh, Mom! We were trying to help you out. You and Daddy are working so hard—"

Mary interrupted. "What you were doing was trying to scare the little girls."

"Well, they should get in trouble because they weren't in bed," the first boy said.

"Then so should you," Mary replied, tipping his chin and looking into his eyes. She let go of his chin and straightened to her full height. "China, Deedee, these scary creatures are my eldest children. This is Travis," she said, gesturing to the boy with his finger in his ear. "And this is Tyler." She turned her attention to the boogie men. "Boys, this is China, and this is Deedee. They're your baby-sitters for the weekend."

The boys looked at each other and said, "Glock bock."

Mary crouched down. "No code language this weekend. It's not fair."

"But Mom—" Travis protested.

"It's like telling us we can't talk for the whole weekend," Tyler finished.

"When no one else is around you can talk however you like. But in front of others, be considerate."

"Yes, Mom," the boys said together.

"Now both of you get into bed before I lose my merciful attitude."

The boys disappeared into the first room and shut the door. Moments later, bumps and thumps sounded like human pinballs bouncing inside the room.

"Twin boys," Mary said. "A challenge and a blessing."

Before China could think of a response—such as "Are you sure it's okay to leave us alone with these kids?"—Mary had reached the second door. She knocked, then opened the door. "How's it going in here?" she asked.

"Fine," a small voice responded.

"I have someone I want you to meet. Two someones."

"Are they twins?"

"No, sweetheart. Friends, but not twins."

"*Good!* I'm sick of twins."

"Alice!" Mary chided.

A small, repentant voice said, "I'm sorry, Mommy."

Mary opened the door to let China and Deedee inside. Toys and books spilled out of open boxes and littered the floor. To get closer to the double bed,

China stepped over naked Barbie dolls and their clothes, a Magna Doodle, a variety of stuffed animals, an old office phone, a Candy Land box with one side torn off, and a number of rainbow-colored plastic ponies and other critters with wispy, tangled hair.

Deedee sat at the foot of the bed on the pink comforter wadded up there. China stood next to her, a smile washing over her face at the sight of the four cherubs lying in the bed.

Mary touched the curly brown head of the first one. "This is Emily."

"Hi, Emily," Deedee said. "How old are you?"

"Seven," Emily said softly. Long lashes fluttered over her wide green eyes. Unlike her brothers, Emily had no freckles.

We'll have no trouble with this one, China thought.

"Emily is learning to read," Mary said. "So she reads to her sisters at night before they go to bed."

"What are you reading?" Deedee asked.

"*Goodnight, Moon,*" Emily said, her voice softer and shier than before.

"These two," Mary said, pointing to a blond next to Emily, and an identical one on the far side of the bed, "are Valerie and Vickie. They're almost two."

Their blue eyes took in China and Deedee as though they were dressed-up characters come to life from a movie. Neither said a word. Valerie moved a board book close to her chest, and Vickie pulled the pink, striped sheet up to her nose.

"Alice is our dramatic child," Mary said, indicating the last little girl.

Alice playfully stuck out her tongue at her mother. China figured she was adopted. She had little fuzzy black ponytails sticking out all over her head. Dark-brown eyes sparkled. Her skin was that creamy chocolate color that made China envious.

"You'll always know when Alice is around," Mary said, reaching over to tweak her nose.

"That's because I have a big voice," Alice said, proving her point. "And I'm five." She held up five fingers for emphasis.

"It's nice to meet you girls," Deedee said. "We've got a lot planned for tomorrow."

"My brothers won't be there, will they?" Alice asked.

China smiled at her. "Sure, we'll have fun with them, too."

Alice rolled her eyes. "You don't know them very well," she said in a sing-song voice.

"Enough," Mary said gently. "It's time for prayers and for Valerie and Vickie to go to their bed."

In voices that softened China's heart, the little girls thanked God for their toys, the trees, each pet by name, and all the water at Camp Crazy Bear that they could play in.

After a rousing "Amen!" the twins tumbled out of bed and ran for their room.

"They never walk anywhere," Mary warned. "They also love to climb. Sometimes they even, uh, finger-paint, if you know what I mean."

China thought that was an odd way to put it. "Sure, we know what you mean."

"I'll show you where the cleaning supplies are, just in case."

"Okay." China wondered at Mary's conspiratorial tone.

A giant "crib" dominated the twins' room. "It's specially made," Mary explained. "Twins are so close in the womb; I couldn't bear for them to be apart until they're ready." She lifted them into the bed. They scooted to one end and waited for Mary to cover them with a sheet. They snuggled next to each other and peaceful looks appeared on their faces.

As Mary turned off the overhead light, a nightlight popped on. "Good night, girls," she said.

"Night, Mommy."

Mary closed the door. "They can get in and out of their crib on their own," Mary warned. "I've told them not to, for their own safety. But sometimes they don't listen. So, no matter what anyone tells you, I'd prefer you lifted them in and out."

Downstairs, Mary indicated that China and Deedee should sit on the green-covered sofa. She placed the rocker in front of them and sat down. Pete moved about the room, unpacking boxes and folding the empty ones flat.

"I'm sure you figured out that Alice is adopted," Mary said. "Valerie and Vickie are also adopted. That's another reason for the unique bed. When they were six months old, they came to us from a difficult home situation. I wanted them to have the constant comfort of each other in spite of the upheaval in their lives."

Pete appeared with iced tea for them all. After handing out the glasses, he took a handkerchief from his pocket and mopped his brow. He went back to his work without saying a word. China was glad. His powerful voice made her want to cringe.

"This weekend shouldn't be difficult," Mary said. "They're good kids. I've written out a schedule for food and sleep to show you what they're used to. But you can vary that. You don't have to be a clone of me. But I do warn you to stick to Valerie and Vickie's nap time. If you don't, you could have a disaster on your hands. They don't do well without their naps.

"The telephone isn't hooked up yet," she continued, "and the television is on order. Ours died right before the move. But I've heard you don't have a television either, so you're used to life without one."

China avoided looking at Deedee. *There went half of our baby-sitting strategy,* she thought.

"Any questions?"

"Where do we sleep?" Deedee asked, her voice diplomatic and businesslike.

"I almost forgot. Our room is at the end of the hall. Clean towels are hanging in the bath."

China had questions. Lots of them. But she couldn't corral any of them. They stampeded through her mind, kicking up dust, and ran into each other.

Deedee shook her head slowly. She had questions, too; China could see them. But Deedee didn't say anything.

"Mary," Pete said, his voice booming, "if you can break away, we should get going. We've got a long drive and a big day tomorrow."

In a few minutes, they were gone.

Deedee and China just sat on the green couch and stared at each other.

CHAPTER SIX

"**I** DON'T THINK IT'S GOING TO BE THAT DIFFICULT," Deedee said brightly, finishing her tea.

China searched her friend's face and looked into her eyes. "You lie," she said.

"Quiet! I'm trying to convince myself."

"I keep telling myself that they're just regular kids."

"Yeah," Deedee said quietly. "But there are so many of them." She picked at the raised design on the green spread beneath her.

"Only one more than you've got at home. Besides, how much trouble can kids get into in such a short period of time?"

Deedee clutched her empty glass. "At least they're sleeping now," she said. "Maybe we should follow their example. We've got a long day tomorrow."

"Are you nuts? It's way too early. We've got popcorn to eat and a game to play."

"What game?"

"Doesn't matter," China said. "Something to lull our minds into thinking all is well and all will be well."

The girls found the popcorn where Mary told them it would be and stuck a bag into the microwave. They cleared a place on the massive dining table and found two decks of cards.

"Nerts!" China said, holding up the two decks. She loved the fast-paced game. It got her adrenaline going and forced her mind to work quickly. Deedee was a good match. She may have been more mellow in her approach to life, but her mind was every bit as quick.

After several rounds of Nerts—complete with slamming cards on the table, shouting, and calling each other foolish names like "Pencil neck!" and "Shoebox head!"—they decided maybe they should check on the kids.

Deedee rummaged through the kitchen drawers and found a toothpick. She turned her back to China and broke it, placing the pieces side-by-side in her hand. Then she held out her hand. "Short one has to check first," she said.

China studied the toothpicks, one sticking up higher than the other. She wondered whether Deedee would try to trick her by making the short one look tall. She chose the shorter one. Deedee grinned. "You lose. I mean, you win." .

China stuck out her tongue. "If I don't come back in 10 minutes, you'd better come looking for me."

China crept up the stairs, doubting the children were asleep. They were probably sneaking around terrorizing each other. Instead of chaos, silence met her. But she wasn't convinced something more sinister wasn't going on. And then she heard it . . . a muffled sound coming from the girls' room. She planted her ear to the door and realized someone was crying.

China pushed open the door. The light from the hallway spilled a path of light into the room, and China saw a little head duck under the covers.

She approached the blob and gently touched it. It squiggled away.

China put her hand firmly on the blob. "What's wrong, Emily?" The blob jerked away harder.

"Can I help you?"

When there was no response but a sniffling sob, China lifted the covers and peeked underneath.

"Do you want your mommy?" China whispered. She wanted to stroke back the hair from Emily's face but was afraid to.

Emily shook her head. "Go away."

"All right," China said.

She went downstairs to the kitchen. "Play solitaire," she told Deedee on her way through. "Emily's crying. I'll talk to her a little and then come down."

"Can I help?"

"I think she's shy enough with just me. If I don't get anywhere, we can trade."

When China entered the bedroom again, nothing had changed. The lump under the covers quivered from the effort of gulping back sobs.

China pulled back the covers and held out a small glass of milk and a chocolate chip cookie. "Here. I brought you something."

Emily almost took the cookie, then pulled back her hand. She looked warily at China's offering. "We're not supposed to have midnight snacks."

China looked at the clock. "Since it's only a little before nine, I'm sure it will be all right."

As Emily nursed the milk and cookie, her lips almost curved into a shy smile. When she was done, she wiped her mouth with the back of her hand.

"It's okay if you miss your mommy," China said, putting the empty glass on the floor.

Emily covered her face with her hands. She curled up into the tiniest ball she could squish her body into.

China perched on the side of the bed. "It's okay if you miss your mommy," she said again. "I miss my mommy."

Emily peered through her fingers at China. "You do?"

China nodded. It struck her that this little girl was like Heather Hamilton, only shrunk down into a tiny body. Trying to be stoic. Not wanting to admit her pain.

Emily frowned. "No, you don't," she said. "Big people don't miss their mommies."

China sighed. She realized she didn't like to think about missing her mom. She nodded. "Yes, I do.

Sometimes I miss her so bad it feels like there's a big orange in my chest. It's all full of orange juice tears. Someone's in there trying hard to squeeze all the tears out, but they just won't come." China felt herself slip into the dark corner of grief where she hated to go. "What I really want is for my mommy to rock me."

Emily looked astounded. "Where is your mommy?"

Emily's voice brought China out of the corner. "She lives way far away in a beautiful country called Guatemala. She and my daddy are missionaries there."

Emily's eyes grew wide. "I know about missionaries," she said, pulling the covers to rest underneath her chin. "My Sunday school teacher told us all about missionaries. They go far away to tell people about God. And they live their whole lives for other people."

China nodded. A wistfulness came over her. "Yeah. I don't get to see my family very much, even when I live close to them." She stopped abruptly, wondering if she should open up to a seven-year-old.

"I don't get to see my parents very much," Emily said, her eyes brimming with tears. "Mommy's always busy taking care of the twins, and Daddy has to work a lot to feed all of us."

China didn't know what to say. All the ideas that popped into her head sounded trite. They had all been said to her over the years. "God is the best parent." "You know your parents love you." "You have the most wonderful parents." "You are so lucky to have parents who serve God." She hated every pat phrase. It didn't matter that they were true.

China touched Emily's hair and said, "It hurts, doesn't it?" China almost choked on her own equally lame statement. She expected Emily to slug her.

Instead, Emily smiled shyly. "Do you pretend you're invisible, too?"

"Invisible?" China stopped stroking Emily's hair.

"Umm-hmm." Emily seemed to perk up. "I pretend I'm invisible so I don't bother anybody."

"I don't think anyone would say you're a bother," China told her. *What a horrible thing to believe!*

Emily nodded emphatically. "My brothers say so all the time."

China chucked her under the chin. "Brothers are supposed to say that," she said with a smile. "That's their job." She changed to her serious, older person mode. "I don't think your parents would ever say that."

"They don't say it, but I know it," Emily said.

"No . . ."

"Yes, I am. I'm another mouth to feed. Another problem for Mommy to take care of. If I'm invisible then maybe they won't be so busy and tired all the time."

China knew Emily's parents loved her. She saw it on their faces. She knew her own parents loved her. But knowing the truth and really believing it deep inside your heart were two different things. She remembered hearing her mom and other missionary women discussing how much there was to do, and the problem of balancing time. It wasn't a problem of being loved or not being loved. It was a matter of time pressures. Even knowing the truth sometimes hurt.

"Do you think your mom and dad love you?" China asked.

Emily nodded her head, her eyes lighting up with the truth she knew and believed.

"Someday maybe you'll find a real good friend and you won't have to be invisible anymore," China said.

Emily crooked her finger for China to come closer. "Will you be my friend?" she asked in a breathy whisper.

"You bet," China whispered back. She tapped Emily on her little pug nose and kissed the top of her head.

China left the room feeling so good inside that she almost floated all the way down the stairs and into the dining room. She sat across the table from Deedee.

"So?" Deedee asked. She flipped over three cards. Not finding a play, she flipped over three more.

China considered telling Deedee everything, then said, "Emily just misses her parents, that's all."

Deedee flipped over the last three cards, then pushed all the cards together. "More Nerts?"

China flashed her competitive smile. "Absolutely!"

A little after 10:00, they grabbed their pack and

duffel and tiptoed upstairs in the quiet house. They paused at each door to peek in at the children. One boy slept on the bottom bunk with his behind way up in the air. The older girls slept on the double bed as far away from each other as possible. The little twins cuddled close.

"They look so precious," China whispered.

"Looks can be deceiving," Deedee said. She leaned on the door jamb. "Let's just hope they're half as precious tomorrow."

"We can do this, Deeds," China said. "It will go fine. This evening went smoothly. I made a new friend. It's going to be fine."

"The evening went smoothly because we didn't have anything to do," Deedee said dryly.

"I think that because we're doing things the right way, everything is going to be just great. God will bless us. You watch."

"This sounds too much like you saying, 'Trust me.'"

China shrugged and moved toward the door at the end of the hall. "Maybe so. But God wouldn't let us down. He's going to make it okay. Even fun. You watch."

China opened the bedroom door. The room looked less put together than any of the others. Stacked boxes created an obstacle course, and the king-sized bed dominated the center of the room. Two old dressers stood with drawers pulled out as though someone had gotten interrupted in the middle of replenishing the drawers.

Deedee dropped her pack on the bed and unzipped it. She found her brush and began to pull it through her thick hair. "What do you think is happening on the houseboat right now?" she asked.

China flopped backward on the bed and stared at the ceiling until it dissolved and became a houseboat. "Probably the same thing that's happening right here. Everyone's getting ready for bed. . . ."

"No, they aren't," Deedee said, dropping her brush onto the bed. She flopped next to China. "They're still up, only they're sitting on the deck."

"Talking in European accents, looking at the stars, laughing at the differences between our lives and theirs."

"I wonder how cute those guys really are," Deedee said.

"I don't even want to think about it," China replied. "If they're as cute as I think they are, we'd both ditch these kids and get there any way we could. Forget Magda!" China shouted, her fist in the air. "How come you don't get any cute guys at Crazy Bear?"

"BT was kinda cute."

"Yeah," China said, "but he's BT. Kissing him would be like kissing your brother."

Deedee wrinkled her nose. "No, thanks." She rolled over. "Maybe only European guys are cute."

"Maybe we're too picky," China suggested.

"True, true," Deedee said. "I know I'm looking for the perfect guy. He's got to be adorable, sweet, romantic. . . ."

"Don't forget fun, smart—"

"And adorable. . . ."

"Deedee! I thought you cared more about what someone is like on the inside."

Deedee pushed off her socks with her toes. "I'm a heathen, okay? I go for looks first, and then if he's cute enough for me to want to follow him everywhere, then I'll decide if he's got all the other stuff I want."

"Stuff?" China squealed. "It sounds like you're looking for a stuffed animal, not a guy."

"Your mind is out of control again," Deedee said, grabbing a pillow and whopping China with it.

"You said it, not me. I can't wait to see how God is going to answer that one," China teased.

"I don't think God is who you think He is," Deedee said thoughtfully, after a long pause.

"Are you turning serious on me?" China asked, getting up from the bed.

Deedee looked at her watch. "It's that time of night. Time for me to get serious." She put her watch on top of the dresser and picked up her brush from the bed.

"Okay, so what do you mean that God isn't who I think He is?" China asked. She put her duffel on the end of the bed and started searching through the chaos to find her sleep shirt and boxers.

"I don't think He smacks us, and I don't think He makes everything okay when we obey Him."

China extracted a wrinkled red shirt with the number 52 on the front. "But He rewards those who obey, right?"

The brush stopped midstroke. Deedee wrinkled her nose. "That's true, but there's something wrong with that statement. I can't put my finger on it right now." She tapped the brush on her hand. "This whole baby-sitting thing has got me thinking."

"*You? Thinking?*" China teased.

"Shut up," Deedee teased back. "Maybe it's because this whole thing was our choice. God didn't have any-thing to do with it." She scrunched her face. "It really is so complicated. We choose, and right or wrong we live with our consequences, right?"

China nodded.

"God doesn't *make* us do anything. We always have free choice."

China held up her hand and said, "But when we do what's wrong, we get punished."

"Or do we? Maybe it's the natural consequences of our choice."

"Deedee, this is too complicated for my poor brain tonight, okay? We'll certainly find out tomorrow." China felt confident that everything would be okay. Her time with Emily was proof. She turned her back to

Deedee as she traded her day shirt for the night one. She'd never gotten over an extreme modesty. Deedee could strip starkers in front of her, but China felt embarrassed even in her underwear. At least Deedee didn't tease her about being modest.

"I hope you're right," Deedee said, hesitantly. She opened all the windows in the room as China crawled into the bed and covered herself with only the sheet.

Even though it was a strange bed, China fell asleep immediately.

CHAPTER SEVEN

A LIGHT, INSISTENT TAPPING dug into China's conscious-ness. She willed the dream to shift in order to get the tapping to stop. It persisted. Suddenly, it stopped, and China felt tiny lips on hers so briefly and fleetingly that it was as though she had been kissed by a butterfly.

"Wake up, Sleeping Beauty," a small voice said. "Wake up!"

China opened her eyes. A bright smile lighted Alice's beautiful face. Her brown eyes stared into China's.

"I thought you'd never wake, Sleeping Beauty. I found your poisoned apple on the table."

Sleep clogged China's brain with cotton. Who was this child? Why was she here? An unseen hand snatched the cotton and she remembered. Baby-sitting. All day. For six kids. *Six!*

"The Seven Dwarfs are making a magic breakfast for you," Alice whispered. "Some is on the floor an' stuff, but I think there will be enough for you, since you're the princess."

China's eyes opened wide. This kid was more into imagination than she was!

"Okay," she said to Alice. "When shall I eat my magic breakfast?"

"I think you should come now," Alice said. She found China's hand and tugged lightly on it.

China rolled over and reached across the expanse of the king-sized bed to tap Deedee. "Deeds. We've been called to duty. Wake up."

Deedee moaned. "You take care of it. I'll do lunch."

"You'll do now, too," China threatened. "Or I'll send them all up to—"

"Okay, okay, I'm awake." Deedee sat up in bed, her balance not in sync yet. She tugged on the scrunchie that attempted to capture her hair for the night. Wisps of wild hair stuck out all over her head. China was used to the sight of the bride of Frankenstein every morning. So the piercing, bloodcurdling scream from Alice caught her off guard.

"It's the wicked one!" screamed Alice. "She's the one who poisoned you. Quick, escape!"

"It's just Deedee," China said. "Her hair . . ."

Alice tugged so hard that China thought her hand would detach from her arm. "All right, I'm coming, Alice."

China stumbled out of bed, following Alice's lead. Outside the bedroom door something had gotten loose. A house tornado, perhaps. A batch of puppies. A silent bomb. Maybe a weird phenomenon had occurred—one China had never heard of before—where one-half of the house tilts, causing all the contents to fall from the bedrooms into the hallway.

Alice wouldn't let China pause even to figure out what had really happened. All China knew was that once where there had been an empty hallway, there was now a tangle of clothes, toys, boxes, and other paraphernalia she couldn't make out in the mess. She picked her way through as best she could.

"It's important you come," Alice insisted.

China wanted to wail, "Why me? Why do I have to be Sleeping Beauty?" She didn't dare mention that Sleeping Beauty and the Seven Dwarfs didn't know each other. Imagination was important, after all.

The stairs had a little less debris, but it was more difficult to navigate them with slippery and pointed stuff underneath her bare feet.

"I've brought Sleeping Beauty!" Alice shouted. "I've awakened her with a kiss, and she has come! So Dwarfs, bring out her queenly breakfast."

"It's not Sleeping Beauty and the Dwarfs, you dope," one of the boys said, jabbing his finger into his ear.

"It's Snow White," the other finished. "Why don't you ever get it straight?"

China felt her hackles rise. "Maybe she doesn't get it straight because it doesn't matter."

"Oooohhhh," the boys said together, and exchanged glances. "Mom found us a bossy one."

China looked from one boy to the other. Both wore short cotton PJs with baseball hats, bats, gloves, and balls pictured all over them. Both had mussed up hair. Nothing seemed to distinguish them from one another. She could swear that even the freckle patterns were the same. However, she didn't have time to stare at their faces to figure out which was which.

"Hi, Emily," she said warmly to the quiet girl at the table. "How are you feeling this morning?"

Emily glanced up long enough to look at China blankly, then looked back down at her cereal. China raised her eyebrows at the change. *Truly like Heather,* she thought.

China opened her mouth to speak again, but movement behind the boys caught her eye. Two little diapered bottoms sat in a pool of milk. Four little hands patted the milk, splattering it inside the open kitchen cabinets and on the walls. Every time they patted the liquid, delighted giggles erupted. China could see hundreds of Cheerios floating like life preservers in a white ocean. Between pats, the girls picked up life preservers and stuck them in their mouths or hair or on their bare chests. China leapt around the boys to stop a Cheerio from going up a nose. The cat lapped at one corner of the spreading pool of milk. She paused to lick her wet paws, then went back to the pool. The girls shrieked in glee when China slipped in the milk and landed next to them on the floor. The bird, perched on the back of a chair, squealed in alarm.

"Cute, real cute," China muttered under her breath.

She looked up to see that all the cabinet doors stood open. Ripped bags of cereal spilled their contents onto the counter and floor. Ritz crackers looked as though they had been the ammunition in some sort of cracker war. Some lay pulverized from having been caught underneath pounding feet. Others lay as far as the ends of the room, evidence of where the players had stood. The rabbit hopped through, making white footprints across the dry section of linoleum.

"How could we have slept through this?" China moaned. She tilted her chin upward. "Deedee! *Deedee!*" She paused, astonished at the one calm figure in the midst of the storm. Emily still sat at the table, placidly eating a bowl of sugared Wheat Puffs as if nothing in the world went on around her. Tyler and Travis had started a new war, spitting Wheat Puffs at each other.

"Hey," China said. "Stop it. Food is for eating, not for throwing." *I sound like my mother!* she thought, astonished. And how many times had she been involved in a mighty food fight?

"We're not throwing," said the boy with the finger in his ear, "we're hooofing."

Another Wheat Puff zipped from his mouth. And he was right. It sounded like *Hooof.*

"Deedee!" China called. "Come here, *now!*"

Sitting in a puddle of cool milk didn't feel so great. It seeped into her boxer shorts and somehow felt different from water. The boys laughed so hard that China thought they'd inhale a Cheerio from across the room. Emily continued to eat her Wheat Puffs without seeming to even notice what happened. And the babies chortled.

Alice tiptoed through the milky pool and took China's hand. "Oh, my dear Princess," she cried. "Whatever has happened?"

"Emily!" China said in desperation. "Can you help me?"

Emily looked up from her bowl. "I'm invisible, remember?"

From upstairs came the sounds of thumping feet, then a gasp as Deedee entered the upstairs hallway. Moments later, she appeared at the kitchen door.

"China! What are you doing?"

China glared at her. "What does it look like I'm doing?"

"I know you want these kids to like you, but do you really have to stoop this low?"

The boys howled again.

"Deeds, do you really think I did this on purpose?" China felt anger starting to churn in her stomach. "I may be crazy, but I'm not *that* crazy."

"Sorry," Deedee said, not sounding terribly sorry.

She sounded more like her brain had kicked into gear. "You go upstairs and change real quick. I'll start cleaning up this mess. When you come back we'll each take a baby and clean her up."

China stood, white rain dripping from her boxer hem. She saluted. "Yes, sir! Drill Sergeant, sir!"

Deedee waved her on and gestured to the boys. "Tyler, Travis, come get the trash can and start picking up these crackers."

The boys saluted China as she left the room holding a kitchen towel to her behind so she wouldn't drip through the whole house.

When China returned to the kitchen, it didn't look like much had changed. Deedee was trying to be firm but patient with the boys, while sopping up milk with a towel. The boys were doing their job . . . sort of. One stood across the room, holding the trash can in his hands while the other attempted to make baskets with the crackers. That wouldn't have been so bad, except they forgot they were cleaning up and began a new war of hurling the crackers at each other.

The babies now had decided that perhaps this wasn't so fun after all. Both wore unhappy looks, their mouths drawn down. They huffed and spluttered until it became a full-blown wail.

China scooped up the nearest damp baby, wondering why she had bothered to change her clothes. She marched upstairs to the bathroom, trying not to think about how they would survive the rest of the day. She was sorry she had even looked at the microwave clock in passing. It was only 7:13.

China turned on the bathwater and stripped the baby of her soggy diaper. She plunked the unhappy girl into the warm water and threw in a few rubber toys lying next to the tub. The little girl grabbed a bear and a whale, the faucet behind her eyes shutting off almost immediately. China found a washcloth and dipped it into the warm water. As she ran the rag over the little girl, Cheerios slid into the tub. Moments later, Deedee appeared with another sodden toddler.

While the twins bathed, China and Deedee stared at each other, at a loss for words.

" 'Everything will go smoothly . . . you'll see,' " Deedee mimicked sarcastically.

"Maybe the worst is over," China said in a weak voice.

"Not another word from you!"

"I'm not your child!"

"I didn't mean it like that. I just want you to stop saying everything's going to be okay when it's not."

"What's wrong with being an optimist?"

"I would rather you looked at things realistically." Deedee gently picked Cheerios from the little girls' hair. "Realize that maybe things won't always be perfect."

"I don't expect things to be perfect." China let her hand dangle in the water and flicked at it with her fingers.

"It seems to me like you think everything in life is supposed to be fun."

China looked at the dimpled knees in the warm bathwater. She couldn't think of what to say to Deedee. She wanted to think of a snappy comeback. Instead, she could think only of what Deedee had said. Did China really feel like that? Was fun all she ever expected out of life? She thought back to her anger at God and Magda. *I was mad because they wouldn't let me have the fun I wanted.* China blushed.

Deedee washed her twin with soap. China copied Deedee. She held the slippery twin with one hand while she washed her with the other.

"How do we know which is which?" China asked.

Deedee shrugged.

"What's your name?" China asked the little girl she was holding.

"Vih-ee," the girl said.

"Val-ee," the one under Deedee's care said.

"If we just dress them differently," Deedee suggested, "then we'll know which is which all day."

China nodded.

"How will we know which boy is which?"

"We'll just ask them," China replied.

"Fat chance they'll tell the truth."

China lifted Vickie from the tub and wrapped her in a large towel. "I may be optimistic, but you are incredibly pessimistic," she said.

"Realistic," Deedee corrected. She tousled Valerie's hair with the towel. Valerie stuck the head of a purple creature into her mouth and held on to it with her teeth. She waggled her head back and forth until Vickie giggled.

China held Vickie on her lap. "Why is it that when someone is optimistic, they are also unrealistic, but when someone is obviously pessimistic, they say they are only being realistic?"

"China, I'm not trying to fight with you."

"I'm not trying to fight with you, either. I'm just getting frustrated. . . ."

Emily appeared in the doorway, breathless. "You'd better come quick . . ." and then she was gone.

Deedee looked at China. "It's my turn," she said, and left the room.

China led the little girls into their bedroom and helped them find clothes. The only problem was, whatever one wanted to wear, the other wanted to wear, too. China tried to get them interested in different clothes. "Come on, girls! Be individuals!" she said gleefully.

Instead, their mouths puckered and threatened to call in the tearful troops.

"Okay, okay," China conceded. "You can wear the same thing if I can pick it out."

She looked through the drawers until she found two matching outfits where one shirt had a stain on the upper left-hand shoulder. It was a bleached spot no bigger than a dime. Vickie put her hands up in the air, and China slid the shirt over her arms. The neck hole of the other shirt had to be stretched over Valerie's head. China thought her ears would have to be amputated before the shirt would actually fit. But she was determined to be able to tell the girls apart all day.

China got the girls occupied with a red and yellow plastic grocery cart, complete with fake food, then picked her way through the hallway debris and ran downstairs to help Deedee. She turned toward the kitchen where Emily and Alice stared into the doorway. Deedee stood barefoot in the leftover milk, hands on her hips. At the other end of the kitchen, the two boys smirked.

Without turning her head, Deedee said to China, "Get these girls upstairs and dressed for the day. These boys have some work to do."

"That's what you think," one boy said.

"Not only do I think it," Deedee retorted, "I *know* it."

China's toenails almost curled at Deedee's tone. "Let's go upstairs," she said softly to Alice and Emily. They eagerly spun on their toes and ran upstairs.

Emily quietly chose her own clothes, acting as though China wasn't even there.

"I thought you said we were friends," China said to her.

"I'm invisible."

"Not to me. I can see your pretty face and hear your voice."

Emily stopped pawing through her clothes and looked at China.

"And I like knowing you're in the room with me." China hoped it didn't sound as cheesy as it felt.

A smile broke across Emily's face. She put on her clothes, not caring that the blue, plaid overall shorts looked rather odd with the shirt spattered with orange flowers.

Alice scrunched her nose. "Ewww, Emily. That's icky."

"Doesn't matter," Emily said.

Alice must have lost that war a long time ago. She didn't bother to pursue the issue. Instead, she searched through a box of clothing, tossing an occasional article into a small pile. From the pile, she put on various combinations of clothing before coming up with an acceptable pair of lavender shorts and a white shirt with a lavender flower in the center of it. "Is this okay?" she asked China, whirling around in front of a full-length mirror propped against the wall.

"It's fine," China said, trying to hold back a laugh.

Vickie and Valerie dug through the Barbie dolls, trying and failing to put on various outfits. While China waited for Emily and Alice to get dressed, she dressed and undressed Barbies at the whim of the two V's.

When Deedee dropped into the room, all she said was, "It's only 8:30."

"You aren't even dressed yet," China reminded her.

"Maybe not. But I got two stubborn boys to mop the kitchen floor."

China's eyes widened. "I'm impressed."

Emily moved close to Deedee and studied her face. "Wow," she said.

"Where are they now?" China asked.

Deedee closed her eyes. "I think they're getting dressed."

"You'd better hurry, then. No time for showers today."

Deedee shook her head. "Pointless to take a shower." She lifted herself off the floor and disappeared into the hallway.

CHAPTER EIGHT

CHINA HANDED EMILY A KEN DOLL. "How should he be dressed for the day?"

"He's got to go to work," Emily said. "He's a missionary."

China smiled. "Then he's got to dress in something that won't make the people around him uncomfortable."

Emily looked at China curiously. "How can something he wears make someone else feel uncomfortable?" she asked.

"Well, in most other countries, the people dress differently than we do."

Emily grinned and then giggled behind her hand. "I've seen pictures of almost naked people in other countries."

China tried to be calm and cool and not turn red. "Uh, yeah. But I think Ken can wear a shirt and pants. He just wouldn't wear a suit or a biking outfit."

"Ooohhh," Emily said, her voice traveling up and down the scale to show she understood.

Emily dressed the Ken doll in a pair of khaki slacks

and a button-up shirt. "Like this?"

"That's fine, Emily."

Emily made the Ken doll go through the motions of a man going to different villages. She talked to the Barbies that Vickie and Valerie played with. She tried to get Alice's attention, but Alice was too busy with a set of horses who snorted and talked and ran around the room.

Emily marched Ken back to the homemade doll-house. "He's coming home from work, and he's very crabby. So he slams the door." She made Ken shut the small door hard.

"Why is he crabby?" China asked.

"Because no one wanted to hear about Jesus today. He's really sad, but he's crabby when he's sad."

China flashed on all the times she was mad at her father for being crabby when he came home after a long trip. She wanted him to be happy to see her. Instead, he went into his room and her mom had to go in and comfort him. She'd hear him say how useless he felt. How pointless all his work was. No one cared. No one wanted to hear about a God they couldn't see or touch or sacrifice to. And China's response was to pout or get crabby back, angry that her father didn't give her what she wanted.

Deedee appeared, her brushed hair pulled back in a scrunchie. She wore cutoff jeans shorts and a dusky green T-shirt. "What are we playing?" she asked.

"Who's playing?" China said. "Someone is teaching me things I should have known long ago."

"I've only been gone 10 minutes."

China looked up. "Out of the mouths of babes. Truth hurts, Deeds."

Deedee cocked her head. "What in the world are you talking about?" She took the Barbie Valerie offered her and stripped it of a fancy dress and put an exercise leotard on it. She handed it back.

"I don't have the freedom to explain," China told her, throwing a glance toward Emily. She slapped her legs and stood up. "We've got to get that mess cleaned up," she said, pointing to the hallway. "What's that noise?"

"I don't know," Deedee said, cocking her head to hear better. "Maybe some sort of power tool."

A high-pitched whine followed a lower pitched one. Then both whines came together in a unison screeching sound.

Deedee's face twisted into a question mark. "Do you think someone is building something?"

"It sounds kind of close," China said. "Did the Macons say anything about construction going on?"

Deedee shook her head slowly. Her eyes glassed over as she thought about the mysterious noises.

Something wasn't right, but China couldn't put her finger on it. She shook her head as if that would dispel the strange feeling inside her.

Deedee looked around at the mess. "Do you think we could get two male types to give us a hand?"

"Good idea." China knocked on the boys' closed door. "Travis, Tyler, we need your help out here."

She waited, but there was no answer. She knocked again, harder this time.

"Travis? Tyler?" She opened the door. "Uh, Deedee? I think we have a problem." China gestured to the empty room.

Deedee shook her head. "Let's go on a boy hunt."

"Okay," China said in her best camp sing-song voice. "Okay, let's go."

"Let's go," they chanted together as they marched down the stairs.

The two girls moved toward the sounds, which seemed to come from the opposite side of the metal storage shed. Four flapping, squawking, unhappy ducks waddled past them as fast as they could go. On the other side of the shed, a small pine tree bore a multitude of what appeared to be fresh holes—from either an overly ambitious woodpecker or someone in control of a drill. The pieces of a sawhorse, neatly disassembled, lay in a pile on the ground.

One of the boys, his back to the girls, danced side to side, waving his arms.

"Come get me, Obie-Wan," he shouted over the whirring noise. "I dare you." He aimed an imaginary laser gun—a power screwdriver—at his enemy. The bit spun and whined in a high-pitched sound.

The other T faced him, holding his own laser weapon—a power drill. He pulled the trigger, and it screamed in response. His arms shook from the weight of it. He looked at "Darth Vadar" with a phony evil grin. "Sure, Darth Vadar, I'll come get you."

China and Deedee looked at each other.

"I don't believe this," China said. She marched toward the T with the drill. "Hey!" she shouted. "You could hurt somebody, you know."

"I know, Princess Leia," he said flatly. "Stay back or it will be you." He put his hand out protectively. "Darth Vadar is an evil, evil man."

"I'm serious," China said, pulling his attention away from his brother.

"So am I," he said with such seriousness that China almost burst out laughing.

She decided to try a different tack. "Obie-Wan, it is foolish to fight Darth Vadar now."

He pointed the drill at her and pulled the trigger. China stepped back from the spinning tool. "Do not interfere, Princess Leia, or you will be in danger, too."

He tried in vain to keep the impish grin off his face. China knew that look well. It was the same look her younger brother got when he thought he was being cute, when in reality he was being stupid.

The big dog stood off to one side, barking incessantly.

China shook her head. Why did boys always seem

to have such grandiose and destructive ideas? "I'm not in any danger," she said boldly. "But you could accidentally drop that thing and put a nice hole in your foot. Now turn it off."

"Why should I?"

"Because I said so," China said with quiet authority. Silently, she screamed to herself, *I sound like my mother! Whatever happened to my vow of explaining things to a kid? I promised myself I would never say to my child, "Because I said so."*

"Whoopdeedoo. I don't have to listen to you." The little boy wiggled his behind in a victory dance, the drill pointed to the sky.

"I suppose I'll have to tell your parents when they get home," she said. *Oh, now that was powerful.*

"Ooohhh. Scare me to death."

China tried to think of something useful to get this kid to put down the potentially body-damaging tool. "How about if I give you something to bore into with that thing?"

"Too late," he said, gesturing with his laser weapon toward the pine tree. "Now I must battle the evil Darth Vadar." A false bravado seemed to seize the kid.

"Oh, no you're not." As soon as China said the words she wished she'd kept her mouth shut. *Challenge a male and watch what happens.*

He faked a lunge at her with the drill spinning, but she stood firm.

When he saw that she wasn't going to play along, he stopped and curled his upper lip. "Aw, you're no fun," he said, and he dropped the drill. By the time it hit the ground, the whirring motor gave way to silence. China ran to pick it up.

"Get off me!" screamed the other T.

China turned to see why T-2 was screaming. The boy lay facedown in the dirt with Deedee on his back. She sat there as calmly as though she were having afternoon tea.

"I'll get off when you decide to listen to me," she said. She held her own trophy—the power screwdriver—in her hand.

"I don't have to listen to you! You're not my mother."

"Get off my brother!" T-1 shouted. "You have no right—"

China stopped him. "And you have a right to come after me with a power drill?"

"Awww, I was just kidding. Only a dummy wouldn't know that."

China turned the drill over in her hand. "Only a dummy would pick up any kind of power tool and turn it on without something specific to work on. No tool should be used for something other than its stated purpose."

"Now you sound like my dad." T-1's freckles scrunched together in a frown.

"Good. Then maybe you'll listen to me," China said, trying to sound sure of herself.

Deedee held the ear of T-2 with her index finger and thumb. "You and your brother are to have time-out in your room for the next hour. Clear? If you say yes, I'll let you up."

The two T's looked at each other. "Sumpta hooda?" T-2 said.

T-1 sighed. "Seenka."

T-2 nodded, and Deedee let him up. China was about to remind them of not talking in their secret language, but somehow they had communicated and decided to give in. She kept quiet.

The T's walked slowly to the house without looking back. The dog trotted after them.

China took the tools and put them in the unlocked shed. Deedee rested her arm on the shed and put her forehead against it.

"Now what, China? They're only gearing up for another battle. How do we get them to behave?"

China shook her head. "You're the one with the experience, not me." She looked around the shed, checking for sharp objects the boys might decide to use on each other or their siblings. There were plenty. She shivered when she spotted a chain saw. She found an open rusted lock and put the hasp through the metal holes of the shed door and locked it.

"Do you know where the key is?" Deedee asked.

"Frankly, I don't care," China said. "They can cut it off if they have to. Better than finding a twin with an extra hole in his body."

"Has your brother ever done anything that stupid?" Deedee asked.

A smile spread across China's face. "My brother has done plenty. So have his friends. My brother fell off a second-floor ledge because he was trying to scare some people one room over from where he was. Dumb!"

"Was he hurt badly?"

"No, just a sprained ankle and some scrapes and stuff."

Deedee shook her head in disbelief. "Is this a guy thing?"

China shrugged.

"Well, what are we going to do right now?"

"I'm going to talk with Magda," China said. "I think she needs a little reality check on her dearest darlings."

"On what phone?"

China gave her an ugly look.

"I wish I could talk with my mother," Deedee said, ignoring China's look. "She manages to keep my brothers in line. I have history with my brothers. They know if I threaten to tell Mom or Dad, I will. And they know the punishment will follow. These kids don't seem to respond to that. Maybe we should call my mom or go get her."

"It would be so much easier if we had a phone, Deedee. And we can't leave just one of us in charge to go talk to your mom. Besides, if they don't listen to us, why would they listen to another person they don't know?"

Deedee's eyes widened, and she gripped China's arm. "Uh-oh. There's no one in charge now."

They raced to the house and flew upstairs. The boys were in their room, already zooming spaceships around. The older girls played with Barbies and listened to a *Psalty* tape. Vickie had made stair steps out of dresser drawers and sat on the top of the dresser, pulling underwear out and throwing it into the air like parachutes to land on the floor. Valerie sat in a packing box, climbed out, then found another she liked better.

Deedee lifted Vickie down from the dresser and closed all the drawers, then put her in an empty box beside her sister. The cat took Vickie's place on the dresser, surveying the scene below.

China plopped down on a pile of stuff in the hallway and sighed. "I'm ready for this to be over," she said.

Deedee checked her watch. "It's only nine o'clock."

China fell backward and closed her eyes. "Wake me when it's over."

"China, what are we going to do here?" Deedee asked softly. She picked up a pair of pants and checked the size in the waistband. She folded it, set it aside, and reached for another article of clothing.

"I don't know," China said, staring at the ceiling. "We've got to get these kids to obey or we're dead."

"Not literally," Deedee said.

"Of course not. But the house could be destroyed. And who would get blamed? We would. These parents would never think their precious, darling children could be such gangsters." China sat up and crawled through the pile of stuff, tossing clothes in Deedee's direction. She put the toys in piles in front of the rooms where she thought they might belong. "All the money we were supposed to earn would go right back into paying for repairs."

Deedee rolled two matching socks into a ball. "I keep thinking about our parents. How do they get us to obey?"

China sat back on her haunches, thinking. "They threaten us."

Deedee stopped her folding. "No, they don't."

"Kinda." China took the debris from the stairs and tossed it into the hallway.

"Like how?"

"If we don't obey, we get some sort of punishment."

"True enough, but we still try if we think we can get away with it."

China sorted some more toys from clothes, trying to think how to put into words her swirling thoughts.

Suddenly, she smacked her forehead. "I know! I obey my parents because I love them, and I don't want to disappoint them."

Deedee nodded slowly. "Too bad we can't get these kids to obey for that reason."

"I obeyed my teachers just because I knew they were my authority. It was just the right thing to do."

Deedee stuck Legos together into one big piece. "This isn't helping, China."

"Just wait. I'm brainstorming." China tried to speed through all the situations where she was supposed to obey someone. She couldn't think of any that applied to their situation right now. "I obey God because I'm scared He'll knock me flat if I disobey."

Deedee smiled. "From my point of view, my own stupid choices are what end up clobbering me," she said. She looked into the girls' bedroom. "Valerie, don't climb up there."

"Look at the Old Testament," China said, working from the other end of the hall. "God does all kinds of things to the Israelites that seem awfully harsh to me. He opens up the earth and swallows some. He sends snakes that kill a bunch. And there was some kind of disease. He just kind of seems to be this angry person ready to lash out at the slightest mistake." She crawled to the end of the hall to deposit four tiny Winnie-the-Pooh shoes at the farthest door.

"What about the New Testament?" Deedee asked.

"Jesus, who is the God we can see, treated sinners with such tenderness. Especially women and children."

"I keep trying to tell myself that," China said. "But I keep seeing this angry man standing there lashing out at all of us knuckleheads here on earth."

Deedee put one stack of folded clothes in front of the boys' door. She put another in front of each of the girls' doors. She retreated to her cleared spot and chose more clothes to fold. "Okay. So let's think about parenting as if we were God doing it. What do we do with these boys?"

China smiled mischievously. "We zap them, of course."

"No," Deedee said. "We put them out with poisonous snakes and let the snakes do the job."

"Maybe we could pray for an earthquake to swallow them," China suggested.

"Seriously . . ." Deedee said.

"I am serious. They're not the least bit sorry."

Deedee sighed. "It's a good thing we're not God, huh? We wouldn't give a chance to anyone who makes our life tough."

China thought about that and knew it was true. She had judged Heather quickly, wanting to bump such a nasty person out of her life if not off the planet altogether. "Okay. Truly seriously. How does God, or our parents, get us to obey?"

Deedee smacked her hands together. "Respect! Our

parents and God have our respect. So when they tell us to do something, we will obey or disobey depending on what we really want."

China smiled. "It was out of respect for Magda and God that we decided to go ahead and baby-sit. That's it, Deedee! You're a genius."

Deedee bowed from her seated position. "Thank you, thank you."

China gathered an armful of clothes and deposited them next to Deedee. The front half of the hallway was now clean. "But how do we make this work? How do we get these kids to respect us?"

"We use the power of their respect for their parents."

"How?"

"We'll call the Macons from a pay phone and let them put some fear into the boys. Then the children's respect for their parents' authority will bleed over onto us."

China nodded slowly. "Let's just hope the kids have some respect for them. Otherwise, we might be the ones who are bleeding."

CHAPTER NINE

WHEN THE GIRLS FINISHED SORTING and folding clothes and putting things away, they called the children together.

"We're going to get shoes on," Deedee announced, "and we're going for a walk."

"I don't want to go for a walk," one of the identically dressed T's said.

"Walks are for babies," the other said.

"We'll go on a hike, then," Deedee suggested.

"I ain't goin' on no hike with my kid sisters," a T said.

China would have loved to slug him right then. *God, can't I be a father like You? I'll just lay him flat right here.* She sighed. She knew God waited and gave many chances before He swooped in. Good thing, too, or she might have been history back when the bears scalped Anna. Or when she disobeyed her own parents, yelling things she shouldn't have, and then didn't feel the least bit remorseful for at least two days—and sometimes she only felt remorse because she wasn't sorry.

Deedee spoke up. "You *will* go with your sisters. You can walk on ahead or behind and pretend you aren't with us. But you can't walk so far away that you can't see us. Got it?"

"I ain't goin'."

"Fine," Deedee said. "You'll miss out on the Chocolate Chip Shakes."

China stared at her. Deedee threw her a look, warning her to keep quiet.

"Oh, all right," the T replied. "If you're going to force us, I guess we have to go."

Deedee turned her back on the boys and rolled her eyes. "Come on, girls, let's get our shoes on."

Deedee picked up the Winnie-the-Pooh shoes and took Vickie and Valerie into their room to dig for socks.

China followed Alice into her room to search for her shoes in the mess. Emily lay Ken down on his bed.

"It's very tiring to be a missionary," she said to no one, and left the room.

Alice changed her clothes, deciding that what she had on was too nice for a hike. She put on a pair of black Lycra shorts with a sunflower on the right leg, and a T-shirt filled to capacity with sunflowers.

"My brothers are such a pain," Alice told China, as she perched a sunflower clip on top of her head. "They're always getting in trouble."

"What do your parents do?" China asked, trying to sound casual.

"They spank them or separate them. But they still get into trouble. Mom says that it's just boys and their age. I think it's twins," Alice said in a grown-up tone.

"Do you know which twin is which?" China asked.

Alice nodded. "They call each other T so that no one knows which is which. But Travis sticks his finger in his ear lotsa times. Mom says it's a bad habit. Dad tries to make him stop. Mom told Daddy once that it makes it easier to tell them apart, so let him do it."

China nodded, trying to keep from throwing her arms around this kid and thanking her. Not that it would make that much difference if they knew which twin was which. But it might throw them off balance just enough to get them moving in the right direction.

Alice put on her shoes. "You know, it's really weird. The Coke doesn't have any bubbles."

"Oh," China said. *What did that mean?*

Bloodcurdling screams startled China, and she jumped to her feet.

"It's just Emily," Alice tried to say. But China was already out the door and down the hall.

"He *hit* me," Emily screamed. "Tyler hit me! Make him stop, make him stop!"

China wrapped her arms around the screaming little girl. "It's okay, sweetie. I'm here. They won't hurt you anymore."

One of the T's—probably Tyler—spoke up. He

looked a little baffled. "She had my Super Screamer Spaceship," he said.

"And that's a good reason to hit her?" China asked, her arms still draped protectively around Emily.

Emily's tears dried and a smug smile flitted across her face so briefly that China would have missed it if she hadn't been at Emily's level. It threw her off.

"Don't hit," China told T, a little less sure of herself. She felt like a piece was missing from this puzzle.

Deedee appeared, twins dangling off each arm. "What happened?"

"I took care of it," China said in a tone she hoped Deedee would catch.

Deedee raised her eyebrows and said nothing more. China would fill her in later.

The walk to Main Camp took longer than either girl could have imagined. The young twins had to be carried part of the way. When they weren't being carried, they ran for the nearest rock or tree and attempted to climb it, or they ran to keep up with their brothers. Alice dawdled; Emily kept to herself. The boys took turns lagging behind or shooting ahead. They talked loudly, often making fun of the girls as if they had no clue who these mindless beings were.

Deedee had to make good on the Chocolate Chip Shakes. She bought three to share all the way around. She and China didn't get much. After the shakes, they gathered the kids around the pay phone.

"I think we should call your parents," China said.

"To tattle on us," Travis said, sticking his finger into his ear.

China felt her face redden at being caught. She hoped these boys were too young to notice body language.

"We thought maybe the girls missed them," Deedee said. "Since you're here, too, you could let them know you're fine."

The boys seemed to accept that.

Deedee took a wrinkled scrap of paper from her pocket. She dialed the number Pete and Mary had left, along with their calling card number.

"Red Lion Inn," came the voice over the line.

"I'd like to speak with Pete or Mary Macon, please."

"One moment."

The phone rang seven times before the hotel operator came back on the line. "I'm sorry. There's no one in the room right now. Would you like to leave a message? I believe they are a part of the seminar that's in progress right now. If it's an emergency, we can stop the seminar and get them to the phone."

Deedee smiled weakly at China. "No, thanks. Just tell them their children called to let them know everything is okay." She hung up the phone.

"Now what?" Deedee asked, sounding completely defeated.

A sneaky smile crept across China's face.

"Don't," Deedee warned.

"No, no. It's nothing bad," China said. "I just think now would be a perfect time to go see Magda, don't you?" She tilted her head and smirked.

Deedee grinned. "Perfect," she said. She turned to the kids. "Do you want to see your daddy's cousin?"

"Yeah!" the girls shouted at once.

"No," the boys said. "That's stupid."

"She works in the camp kitchen," China bribed. "She's always passing out goodies."

The boys looked at each other. "You makin' us go?"

Deedee nodded.

"Yep," China said.

"Then I guess we hafta."

China and Deedee went the back way so the children wouldn't go crazy at the sight of Little Bear Lake and want to play in the water.

Magda threw up her arms when she answered the knock at the back door. "My favorite people in the entire world!" she cried. She gave each girl her own hug but hugged the boys together. "You can't escape Auntie Magda's hugs," she said to the cringing boys.

"You're not our aunt," Tyler told her.

"Well, it's less confusing than saying 'second cousin' all the time. I'm old enough to be your aunt, and I'm bossy enough, too. So you just quit that kind of talk and be respectful."

Two sets of eyes grew wide.

"If I hear you're givin' these gals a bad time, you'll hear from me."

Magda didn't realize she held a rolling pin in her hand. Or maybe she did. Either way, the boys' eyes grew even wider, and they nodded their heads.

China and Deedee exchanged looks that said, *We should have done this hours ago!*

Magda took off after the twins, who ran shrieking around the work table. Alice climbed onto a stool and picked grated cheese out of a bowl, chattering about the wicked stepmother making her do terrible things. Emily sat near the walk-in refrigerator and watched Rick come waltzing through the kitchen, a huge mixing bowl in his arms, singing, "Just a spoonful of sugar . . ."

Magda swooped up one giggling tot and then another and whirled them around as Rick sang.

China bit her bottom lip. "I sure miss this place."

"Cookies all around!" Magda declared, popping open the walk-in door, and letting the boys "ooh" and "ahh" over a refrigerator big enough to be their fort. She rummaged around behind some huge cans and found the bag of leftover peanut butter cookies.

In short order, crumbs scattered across the floor, Magda hugged them all and shooed them out the back door so she could get lunch ready for the high school crowd. She grabbed China and gave her a second hug. "I was mad 'cause I thought you let me down, China honey. You keep bein' that special kid I know."

China closed the screen door gently, feeling horrible inside. She almost wished Magda was still mad at her.

"That lady is nuts!" Tyler said, wagging his head.

Travis trailed a stick along in the dirt. He absently wiped crumbs from his mouth with the back of his filthy hand. "Good cookies, though, T."

China slapped her forehead. "We forgot to let Magda know what monsters these little guys are," she whispered to Deedee.

Deedee's shoulders slumped. "Too late now," she said. "Magda can whip those boys into shape in nothing flat. You think she'll believe we can't control them?"

"I don't like walking in the woods," Alice said, slipping her hand into Deedee's. "It's spooky. And there're bears out there."

"No, there're not," one T said.

"Yes, there are," Deedee said.

"Aww, you don't know nothin'," T replied.

Deedee bit her lip and looked away. China felt her heart skip a beat. Neither girl said any more about bears.

"I'm hungee," Valerie said.

"Me, too," Vickie said.

"After those cookies?" China asked.

"We'll fix lunch as soon as we get home," Deedee told them.

Emily moved next to China. "Friends hold hands

when they walk," she told her.

"That's right, they do," China said, as she lifted Vickie in one arm and reached for Emily's hand with the other.

Emily looked up at China and gave her an adoring smile. "Best friends always?"

"Always," China said.

Back at the house, the boys seemed to have toned down quite a bit.

"Maybe Magda was the answer," China whispered to Deedee.

Deedee responded by holding up crossed fingers. "I hope it wasn't just the walk that mellowed them out." She snapped her fingers, her eyes lighting up with an idea. "Travis, Tyler," Deedee said, "how about watching the twins out here while we fix lunch?"

"Okay," they said eagerly.

"Want to go see the duckies?" one T asked the little ones.

Both girls nodded exuberantly. "Duckies!" they shouted. "Go see duckies!" They tugged on their brothers' hands.

"You sure this is a good idea?" China asked Deedee.

"My mom gives us responsibility to help us act better. It works with my brothers."

"Every single time?"

Deedee looked at China as if she were crazy. "No. But it's worth a try."

"If I hear a power drill, I'm outta here," China said.

Deedee ignored her. "Emily, Alice, will you please help us with lunch?"

"I guess," Emily said, throwing longing looks in the direction of the boys.

China and Deedee made an assembly line with a loaf of bread, peanut butter, jelly, and a table knife. Alice took out two pieces of bread, Deedee spread the peanut butter, China spread the jelly, and Emily stood tall and proud, given the job of cutting the sandwiches in half.

"Am I a bad girl?" Emily asked.

"Why would you think that?" China said.

"Because my mom doesn't like me to help her in the kitchen. So I must be bad 'cause she doesn't want to be with me."

"Oh, sweetie, she wants to be with you. It's just that parents have lots of things to do. They don't get to play all day like kids do. They have lots of things to do to take care of you."

"And sometimes," Deedee said, "moms are so busy that it's easier to do something all by themselves than to show someone else how to do it."

"I could help Mommy," Emily told her. "I would really be a big help." She scrunched up her little face as she tried to carefully line up the knife to cut the sandwich in perfect halves.

"You could be a big help by keeping your room

clean," Deedee said, knowing that's what her own mom wanted the kids to do.

Emily frowned. "I want to help Mommy. I don't want to do boring stuff."

China felt little stab wounds in her conscience. So many times she had gotten mad at her mother for not being there for her. How many times had she really listened to her mother and done what her mother asked without arguing?

"How much more time would my mother have been able to spend with me if I had helped her the way she wanted?" China said softly.

Deedee nodded, startling China.

"I'm sorry," China said, blushing. "I hadn't meant to say it out loud."

"It's okay," Deedee said. "You're preaching to those of us who need to hear it."

Emily scowled at both of them. "You guys just don't understand," she said. She slammed down the knife and stomped off.

China gave Deedee a wry look. "That face—"

"—and voice," Deedee added.

"—were just a little too familiar."

They put the sandwiches on paper plates with a handful of potato chips, poured lemonade into cups, then sent Alice to gather in the twins.

Moments later, Alice ran back to the house. "There's monsters!" she shrieked. "Coming this way! Everyone hide!" She dove behind the back door and giggled every so often.

Sure enough, monsters approached. China tilted her head, as if that would help her see the approaching children more clearly. The tiny girls walked stiff-legged with their arms stretched out in front of them, egged on by their giggling brothers. China couldn't figure out what kind of mask the girls wore.

Emily walked into the kitchen as if she'd never left. "Where did they get those ooky green masks?" she asked.

The fact that Emily hadn't seen the masks before made China a little nervous.

"I thought it was mud," Deedee said.

"Green mud?" China asked.

"Rrrrrr . . ." Vickie growled, as ferociously as her tiny voice could muster.

"Be scared," Valerie demanded.

"I'm so, so scared!" Alice said, peeking from behind the door. "Don't get me, monsters, don't get me!"

China put her hand over her heart. "Oh, my. I am so scared."

Deedee put the back of her hand to her forehead. "Me, too! We'd better run!"

At that, the little twins charged toward the back door. A peculiar odor wafted from them.

China stopped running and wrinkled her nose.

"What is that smell?" Deedee asked.

The little girls came inside the house. "We paint face," Valerie said.

"Green face," Vickie said. "Monsters."

"I see that," Deedee said. "But what did you paint your face with?"

"Green," Vickie said.

"Tyler, Travis . . ." China said, facing them. "What did your sisters paint their faces with?"

"Green . . ." T-1 said, trying hard not to laugh.

"Paint . . ." T-2 said, starting to laugh so hard that his breath came out like foghorn blasts.

Deedee swiped her index finger across one gooey face and sniffed. "*Travis!*" Deedee said as one boy stuck his finger in his ear. "What is this stuff?"

China retrieved her own sample and almost gagged. "It's some kind of smelly gunk," she said.

"Pond slime," Tyler said through his laughter. "The girls thought it was green paint stuck to the side of the pond, and we didn't want to squash their imagination."

Travis nodded emphatically. "Our parents always tell us that we're not supposed to squash the girls' imaginations."

China stuck her hand under the running water in the kitchen sink until it grew hot. She added soap and scrubbed vigorously. "I would doubt this is the kind of imagination they would encourage," she said.

Tyler shrugged. "How were we supposed to know?" he asked in an innocent voice, choking back not-so-innocent laughter.

Deedee washed her hands. "Sit down and eat," she said.

Emily looked up at them, her face sweet and calm. "We usually pray."

"Go ahead," Deedee said, her voice on edge.

"Dear God," Emily began, "thank You for this food. And please help us all to be very good. Amen."

"*Amen!*" China and Deedee repeated.

CHAPTER TEN

"**C**OME ON, LITTLE MONSTERS," China said, holding out her hand to the twins. "We need to clean you up."

"I'm hungee," Vickie said. "I wanna eat."

"You can eat after we get your faces washed."

Deedee took Valerie's hand. "You, too."

"Don' wanna go," Vickie cried.

China picked her up, ignoring the increasing volume of Vickie's screams. China's head started to pound halfway through trying to wash off the sticky green stuff. Worst of all, the little darling wasn't the least bit appreciative of the messy, stinky, hard work China did on her behalf.

"I'm learning a lesson, Deedee," China shouted over the dual screams. The cat sat on the toilet seat, tail slowly twitching, observing it all as if taking mental notes.

"What?"

"Not to have kids."

"I already learned that one," Deedee said, trying to catch a wildly wiggling face with her washcloth.

110

"Kids suddenly have all kinds of energy when all you want to do is clean them," China remarked.

A round face with huge, sad eyes appeared in the doorway. "I liked you," Alice said. "But you're making my sisters scream." She turned around and walked away. She came back moments later. "How come the Coke doesn't have any bubbles?"

"I don't know," Deedee said through clenched teeth, paying more attention to the squiggling child on her lap. "We'll figure it out later."

Downstairs in the kitchen, Corky lay panting on her fluffy side, jelly hanging from her white jowl fur.

"I could swear that dog is smiling," China said.

"No doubt." Deedee pointed to the plates. "There're no sandwiches left."

China sat the girls in their booster seats and put some chips in front of each girl. "Sit, Deeds. I'll make more sandwiches."

The one thing a large family seemed to have was plenty of bread and cereal. At China's house, the bread would have been down to a couple of moldy heels by now. She suddenly remembered they were supposed to give the children their vitamins at breakfast, so she took down the bottle and shook out two for the little girls.

It didn't take her long to make the crustless sandwiches for the tiny twins. They managed to eat their sandwiches and get half of the filling across their faces.

"Oh, joy," Deedee said, "we get to clean their faces again."

China looked around to make sure no one else was listening. "I bet if we set them on the floor for a few minutes, the dogs will clean 'em for us."

"*China!*" Deedee said in horror. Then she relaxed a bit and looked around. "Maybe it's not such a bad idea after all. At least we won't be accused of child abuse."

Alice appeared, smiling at them. "I don't think goldfish like Jell-O," she said calmly, then walked away.

"What was that about?" Deedee asked.

"Maybe we don't want to know."

Deedee dropped her sandwich and stared out the window. "China, did you see that?"

"Of course I didn't. I'm not facing that way."

"I mean, look, would you?"

China took a bite of her sandwich and turned around. She stared out the window and then turned back to look at Deedee. "I didn't see anything."

"There!"

China spun around. Nothing.

Deedee jabbed her sandwich toward China. "Please turn around and keep looking until I tell you to stop."

"Who is going to make sure these precious darlings don't feed their sandwiches to the dogs?"

"I will," Deedee promised. "Now look! Tell me if I'm seeing things."

China ate her sandwich, drinking lemonade between

bites. Then she saw it. A flash of light and something white floating to the ground.

"What is that?" Deedee asked.

"Oh, no . . ." China suddenly realized what was happening. She shoved the vitamins she'd been holding underneath her hand toward the girls. "Here're your vitamins. Don't feed them to the dogs."

She took off up the stairs, Deedee close on her heels.

The door to the boys' bedroom flew open, and China rushed in. The boys didn't have time to react. In one T's hand was a paper airplane; in the other's was a butane lighter.

"What are you boys doing?" Deedee shrieked.

"Playing World War II," Travis said, sticking his finger into his ear.

"Japanese kamikaze pilots," Tyler said.

"You're lighting those on fire?" China asked, so shocked she was actually calm.

"Sure," Tyler said. "But they don't stay on fire all the way down. We haven't figured that part out yet. They always blow out before they reach the ground."

"You could start a forest fire!"

"Or burn down your house," Deedee added. "One spark hits pine needles and—*poof!*—you've got a fire."

"Cool," the boys said, giving each other a thumbs-up.

Deedee flopped onto the lower bunk bed and covered her face.

"It's yucky," said a small voice at the door.

Valerie walked in, holding her pudgy hand out toward them.

China went over and looked at the slimy purple lump the child held. "It's your vitamin, sweetie. You need to eat it."

"It's yucky," Valerie said, tears coming to her eyes.

China got down, face-to-face with her. "It's good for you. Now put it in your mouth."

Valerie put the vitamin in her mouth.

"Now bite it."

Valerie did as she was told.

China thought it sounded odd . . . and it didn't smell sweet. "Wait," she said, sticking out her hand. "Spit it out."

Purple fragments splattered on China's hand. China sniffed it and felt dismay pour over her.

"I'm an unfit mother, Deedee," she cried. She held her hand out to Deedee. "It's purple *chalk.*"

"Where'd you get this?" Deedee asked Valerie.

China answered for her. "There's a chalkboard downstairs in the kitchen. I didn't see any chalk on the tray, but there must have been one piece."

Alice poked her head into the room. "I told you, goldfish don't like Jell-O. If you don't believe me, ask them."

"Okay," Tyler said to Travis. "We can do it this time."

"*No!*" Deedee shouted, spinning around. She

grabbed the butane lighter. "No more kamikaze pilots."

"How about downed MIGs?"

"No planes. No fire. I'll have Magda come over," she threatened.

Tyler slammed his mouth shut, defiance still stiffening his body.

Emily walked in, tears on her face. "I went potty, but the straps fell in."

China looked over Emily's shoulder. Two damp suspenders dangled behind her.

Deedee sighed. "I'll help you find something else to wear." She took Emily's hand and led her from the room.

"Where's Vickie?" China said.

No one answered, so China ran back down the stairs. Vickie sat on the floor, laughing, while Corky licked her face.

Amelia the rabbit hopped by, paused to watch the dog, then continued on her hippity journey.

China lay down on the floor. "God," she said, "I think I'm done here."

Deedee had followed China and now stood over her and stared into her face. "What was that I heard once a long time ago? Was it something about obeying? Yeah, that was it. Since these two girls were obeying God, the job they had to do would be a lot easier."

"So kill me already," China moaned. "I'm half dead anyway."

Alice twirled in front of them. "Don't I look pretty?"

China caught the back of her. She'd changed into a beautiful red velvet dress. A giant satin bow dangled to one side since she couldn't fasten it herself. The red of the dress seemed more intensified by the deep, rich color of her skin.

"You look gor—" China was saying, as Alice spun around.

Bright red lipstick colored not only Alice's lips but much of her face. Lipstick spotted her teeth and her right ear. Face powder lightened her beautiful dark skin to a ghastly pasty color. Mascara darkened her eye sockets rather than her lashes.

"Uh, very nice," Deedee said.

China stared at Deedee, wondering what in the world she was doing.

"My mommy has nice makeup," Alice said. "When she goes out to look pretty, she puts it on."

"Did she say you could put it on?" Deedee asked gently.

Alice pressed her lips together, thinking. "She wasn't here to ask," she said. "I wanted to look pretty for you."

"That's nice," Deedee said. She held Alice's arms and looked deep into her eyes. "But you know what?"

Alice shook her head, mesmerized by Deedee's eyes.

"I like the Alice without makeup much better."

"You do?" Alice's brown eyes opened wide.

Deedee nodded solemnly. "Yes, I do. I think she's the prettiest five-year-old I know."

Alice looked thoughtful. "Then I guess I'd better go find her."

"I can help if you want," Deedee told her.

"Okay."

China fell back on the floor, then the alarm went off in her head. "Naps. We've got to get the little ones to bed."

She picked up Vickie and headed upstairs. Vickie's bottom felt awfully soggy.

"I can't believe it," China muttered to herself. "We forgot to change their diapers!"

China hadn't changed many diapers in her time, but figured it couldn't be all that hard. Once on the changing table, Vickie squirmed and tried to roll over. China leaned on her to keep her still. She found a clean diaper in a plastic package.

"I'm sorry, Vickie," China said. "Your buns are all red now." China didn't know what to do, so she took a wet wipe and ran it over the red skin. She held the clean diaper, not sure which end to stick underneath the little girl. She finally figured it out.

China stuck Vickie in the double crib with a board book and went to find Valerie. She followed the sound of boys' voices and Valerie's giggle to their parents' room.

"Your turn," one T said.

"It tickles," Valerie told them.

China flopped on the bed and looked over the other side. Valerie's face was covered in multicolored O's. One T took another Lifesaver from a pack, licked it, then stuck it on her forehead.

"Should we put them in her hair, too?" T-2 asked.

"I should think not!" China said.

"Oops," T-2 said. "The vice squad has arrived."

"I have indeed. Come on, guys. Get out. Find something else to do that doesn't involve your sisters' faces."

"You're not so scary, you know," T-1 said, then stuck his finger in his ear.

"I know, Travis. But you haven't really gotten to know me yet."

"I'm not Travis," he said.

"Sure you are. Or I'm the Easter bunny. Now scram."

China changed the second sopping diaper and plopped the second twin in her bed. "It's nap time." *For me, too,* China thought.

CHAPTER ELEVEN

Deedee met China in the hallway. A freshly scrubbed Alice ran past them down the stairs.

"My parents used to make us take naps whether we were tired or not," Deedee told China. "I recently found out they didn't care if we slept or not. It was just so they could rest."

"Sounds good to me," China said. "If I stand still too long, I think I'll drop."

Deedee opened the boys' door. The big dog raced past, the bird clinging to his back. "You get to have a one-hour quiet time," she told the boys.

"Says who?"

"Says your mother," China blurted.

"Prove it."

"She wrote me a letter."

"Ha!"

"You made it into a paper airplane and sent it to a fiery death," China said.

"Oh."

China blinked. *It worked!* "So be quiet. We'll be back

119

for you in one hour." She closed the door quickly.

"You lied," Deedee hissed.

"It worked," China said meekly.

"If they find out, that's the end. That's one thing my parents always say. You've got to be honest and do what you say you're going to do."

"Okay," China said, wishing she felt even a little bit guilty.

Deedee went to the top of the staircase. "Emily! Alice! It's time for a rest."

"Don't want one," Emily called with false sweetness. "Don't need one."

"You get one anyway," Deedee called back just as sweetly.

Alice came up the stairs, wiping her mouth. "I wonder why the Coke doesn't have bubbles."

"It went flat?" China suggested.

"I really don't think the goldfish like Jell-O," she added, her face pulled together in a frown.

"I'll check into it," Deedee promised. "Now let's get in bed with some books."

"I want a story tape," Alice told her.

"Okay, a story tape it is."

Emily came upstairs. She glared at the baby-sitters as she went into her room. "I thought we were friends," she muttered, with an accusing look toward China.

China stopped her and knelt down. "We are,

sweetie. I just need some rest so I won't be crabby all afternoon."

Emily looked thoughtful. "Okay. But I don't have to sleep?"

"No, just be quiet," China said. "For one hour. We'll come get you."

The door closed. China and Deedee exchanged weak smiles and tiptoed downstairs. They collapsed on separate sofas. "Should we set a timer?" Deedee asked.

"You can," China said, her eyes closed. "I'm not moving for one whole blissful, sweet, peaceful hour."

⤙

From some distant land came a small voice. "Wake up, Sleeping Beauty."

China felt drugged. She tried to pull her mind from the dark pit. But her mind didn't want to come.

"Oh, Sleeping Beauty," the small voice said, "it's happened again. You must wake up. You *must!*"

Suddenly, China remembered the voice. She forced herself to sit up. "Deedee," she managed to say, "something's happened."

Deedee rolled upright, her hair sticking out all over in the back.

"What is it, Alice?" China asked.

"I've been trying to tell you. The Coke doesn't have bubbles and the fish don't like Jell-O."

China dropped her head forward and stared at

Alice. "You woke me up for that?"

"Well, somebody had to," Alice said. "Besides, the stuff came back."

"What stuff?"

Alice put her hands on her hips and sighed deeply. "The hallway stuff. I woke up, and it was all there again. How does it happen?"

"I don't believe it!" Deedee said, as she looked at her watch. "China! We've been asleep for over an hour!"

"I guess we'd better release the prisoners."

Upstairs they found the hallway full of clothing again. This time all the stuff belonged to the parents.

China stuck her head into their bedroom. The dresser had been tipped over and all the drawers dumped. She put her hand to her head. "I don't even believe this."

Deedee looked over her shoulder. "Whoa!"

A small person tugged on China's shirt. "There's a bear trail outside." It was Emily with a book still in her hand.

"What do you mean?"

"The boys wanted to prove there were no bears, so they put out a dog food trail, hoping bears would come."

"Are you sure?" Deedee asked.

"Come on and see," Emily said.

"No," China breathed. "We believe you. Why don't you go play now."

Emily looked disappointed, but turned around and walked away. "My baby-sitters might as well be missionaries for all the attention they pay me."

Zing, China said to herself.

"We've got to do something with these boys," Deedee said. "But what?"

China felt overwhelmed with all the directions she needed to go at once. Take care of Emily, discover what Alice was talking about, watch the twins, discipline the boys. . . . Is this what her mother faced? Is this why she was crabby for no reason sometimes? Maybe she did have a reason but couldn't explain it all to her kids.

"What's your idea?" Deedee asked. "I can see something on your face, but I can't read it."

"Guilt," China told her. "As for the boys, maybe we should lock them in the shed with the power tools. It would serve them right."

"Or staple them to the wall," Deedee said.

"That's it!" China cried. "We can staple them to the wall!"

"I was only kidding," Deedee said, patting China on the shoulder.

"Well, I'm not."

"You're out of your mind," Deedee said. "First of all, they'd probably enjoy it. Second of all, their parents would kill us."

"No. Listen. These kids think we can't do anything to

them, that any punishment we threaten is no big deal. If we threaten we'll staple them to the wall and they don't believe us, once they break the rules and actually get stapled to the wall, they'll truly believe us. Whatever we say after that will hold quite a bit of weight!"

"Why don't we first go see what the terrible T's have to say about the mess," Deedee suggested.

The two T's were playing quietly with their cars. China's mind did a quick spin. She brought it back under control.

"Can we come out now?" one T asked.

"I thought we were supposed to be quiet," the other said. "But it was awfully noisy."

"Yeah, right," China said.

"What happened out here?" Deedee asked, gesturing to the hallway.

One T shrugged. "Don't know."

China felt her anger swell. With each word of denial, she felt like another puff was being blown into an already overinflated balloon.

"The dresser?" Deedee asked.

"What dresser?"

"Stay here. Don't go away," China warned. She grabbed Deedee's arm. Downstairs they passed the fishbowl. China stopped and pointed.

Beside the fishbowl sat a box of cherry Jell-O. The fish water had turned a nice bright cherry red. "The fish don't like Jell-O," China muttered.

"Apparently not," Deedee said.

Both girls looked at the fish floating upside down.

"The bear trail?" Deedee asked.

"Let's go see."

China braced herself, knowing that although the troublesome bear brothers were gone, it didn't mean more bears hadn't come to take their place. She didn't want to see bears again. Not without bars between her and them. Seeing those blazing eyes of hunger inches from her own nose earlier that summer was an experience she didn't want to repeat.

Deedee bravely opened the back door. Instead of bears, they were met by happy and full dogs. The big one gave them each a generous lick and went back to sniffing the ground for more free food. The small furry one bounded beyond the trees, yapping as he went. The cat squeezed through China's legs and stretched one rear leg, then another, her tail up.

"No bears out here," Deedee said.

"The intent was still there," China said darkly.

China took the stairs two at a time. At the bedroom door, she put her hands on her hips and stared at the boys. "Well, you guys have had quite an active nap time, haven't you?"

The boys looked at each other, then at China. "I thought you said it was okay to play as long as we were quiet," Travis said, the telltale finger exiting his ear.

"I guess you were quiet," China conceded.

Deedee stood next to her. "You can also clean up every mess you made."

The boys looked around them at the few cars, spaceships, and plastic men scattered about the room. "Yeah, okay."

"What?" China almost yelled. "You decide to obey now that you've practically destroyed things, killed three fish, and made a mess of the house? What kind of game are you playing?"

Tyler's eyes narrowed. "What kind of game are we playing? What are you talking about?"

Deedee ticked things off on her fingers. "The dresser. The hallway. The fish. The bear trail."

"Bear trail?" Travis said. "Cool. Too bad there're no bears."

"There are bears," China said.

"That's beside the point," Deedee interrupted. "The point is, you guys made a total mess, and now you get to clean it up."

"We didn't make the mess," Tyler said, "so we're not cleaning up."

"I bet it was that creep Emily," Travis said to his brother.

"Yeah. She always does stuff and blames it on us."

China shook her head. "I can't believe you'd pin it on Emily. She couldn't think of that kind of mischief if her life depended on it."

"Ha!" Tyler scoffed.

"So what are you going to do to us if we don't clean up?" Travis asked, his voice as defiant as ever.

"Staple gun you to the wall," Deedee said.

China's eyes popped open in surprise.

The boys looked at each other, their faces showing curiosity. "You wouldn't," Travis said.

"I've already done it," China said. "Her name was Heather."

"Was?" The boys looked at each other warily.

"We'll give you some time to think about it," Deedee said. "I hear the twins stirring. We'd better get them up."

The girls closed the door behind them and high-fived each other. "That's the trick!" China said. "Win by intimidation."

"I suppose that's how God commands respect," Deedee said thoughtfully.

"Maybe we can get them all finger-painting this afternoon," China suggested brightly. "Didn't Mrs. Macon say they sometimes did that?"

"I didn't see any paints," Deedee said. "But we could look."

They opened the door to the twins' room and froze. "This isn't happening," China said to Deedee. "Please tell me this isn't happening."

"If I said that," Deedee said, "it would be a lie." She looked around the room in astonishment. "It's already happened."

CHAPTER TWELVE

CHINA STAGGERED INTO THE ROOM. "I guess this explains why Mrs. Macon acted so strange when we said what we did about finger-painting," she said.

The babies, in their crib, happily chattered to one another in their own language.

"Mom told me some kids did this," Deedee said. "But I didn't really believe her. Baby poop all over the walls . . . all over each other . . ."

"At least they stayed in bed," China said.

"I'll go run the bath," Deedee said wearily.

Alice, who had a knack for showing up at crime scenes, walked in and surveyed the situation. "Pew," she said. "It doesn't smell very nice in here."

"No, it doesn't," China said.

"I don't feel very good," Alice said.

"I don't suppose anyone would feel very good in here. Why don't you go try to find something we can all do together after we clean up in here."

"Okay. Will that make my tummy feel better?"

"I'm sure it will, sweetheart."

China didn't know where to begin cleaning up. She opened the two windows and prayed for a breeze to break the still, hot air. She moved the crib away from the walls, so the girls couldn't do any more damage and then waited until the bathwater was ready. At least the twins liked the warm bathwater where they could play with floaty toys. Deedee stayed with them while China found Lysol, a bucket, and a rag to wash down the walls and crib.

The cleansed, diapered, and redressed twins laughed their way down the stairs. They ran to the kitchen and climbed into their booster seats, waiting for a snack. China found graham crackers and offered them to anyone who came near. Emily sat at the table eating neatly. She even tidied up after herself by picking up all the crumbs with a damp index finger and sticking it into her mouth.

China crouched next to her. "I really care a lot about you, Emily. It's tough being available for everyone at once."

Emily looked at her sadly, then walked away without a word.

Alice shook her head no when offered a graham cracker. "The Coke still doesn't have any bubbles," she said softly.

China nodded absently.

The cockatiel flew onto the table and strutted like a little man without arms. He squealed and squealed.

"What does he want?" China asked.

"He likes Fruit Loops," Emily said. "The orange ones."

China went to the cereal cabinet and found a bag of Fruit Loops. She carefully dug out the orange ones and put some on the table. Romeo made a funny two-tone chirp that almost sounded like "Thank you," then stabbed at the pieces of cereal, making crumbs fly everywhere. The little twins giggled and offered him graham crackers, which he refused.

"Does the rabbit get a snack, too?" China asked, as the bunny came hippity-hop into the kitchen.

"Of course," Emily said. "A piece of apple."

Inside the refrigerator, China found a sliced apple in a baggie. She took out a browned slice and set it on the floor.

"The dogs?" China asked, now thinking the whole family snacked at the same time of day.

Emily nodded. "One Milk Bone. Inside that cabinet in the box."

The dogs, eager as they were, took the treats gently from China's hand. China wondered how this family could afford to feed all these mouths.

China sighed. "The cat?"

Emily shook her head. "No. She gets to eat when-ever she wants. So she doesn't get a snack. Unless we open a can of tuna. Then she gets to lick the can."

Deedee came in and sat at the table. "I took care of the fish."

"How?" China asked.

Deedee looked around the table, making sure no child was watching, and then said, "John," and motioned with her hand like she was flushing a toilet.

"Oh," China said, and nodded.

"They don't like Jell-O," Alice said solemnly.

"No, they don't," Deedee replied, patting her hair. She took a graham cracker from the package and ate it.

"Can we play beauty shop?" Alice asked. "You sit on the sofa and we pretend to wash your hair and put things in it and make it pretty. Emily can braid."

China sent Alice and Emily to gather their beauty supplies and watched as Deedee washed the little girls' hands and faces, pretending the washcloth was a silly monster coming to kiss their faces.

China smiled. "No screams this time."

"I'm learning," Deedee said.

"I wish we could learn what to do about those boys."

"They're changing tactics," Deedee said. "From wild crazies to more normal, irritating males. This makes me wonder what they're up to more than anything else." Deedee turned her attention to the little girls. "Why don't you two go choose some books for China and I to read to you."

The little girls climbed down from their boosters and ran from the room.

"We still haven't figured out how to get respect from them," China said. "We've managed to bribe them and intimidate them, but I don't think that's quite right."

Deedee sighed. "Me neither. God gets respect because He's big."

"And we're not much bigger than those boys."

"Also because He's so mighty," Deedee added.

"And we're just a couple of pansy girls in these boys' eyes."

"God knows our hearts, so we know we can't hide anything from Him."

Now it was China's turn to sigh. "And those boys could be dismantling the house even as we speak, and we wouldn't even know it."

They looked at each other. "We'd better go check on them," Deedee said.

Emily and Alice were scrounging in the bathroom as China and Deedee passed by. The boys weren't in their room or in either of the girls' rooms.

"Look," Deedee said, pointing at the two dogs who stood at the parents' room, wagging their tails.

"What are you doing?" China said as she stormed into the room.

The dresser had been put in its upright position, the drawers replaced. One T had the telephone to his ear, his eyes wide. The other T lay on the floor, his feet resting up on the side of the bed.

The first T said into the phone, "Uh, wait a second. Here's the baby-sitter." He looked at Deedee and held out the receiver. "They want to talk to my parents."

"Funny joke, guys," China said.

Deedee held the receiver to her ear. "Hello?" she said cautiously. She nodded, then said, "What city am I speaking to?" Her face paled. "What country?" She sank onto the floor. "I'd better go. I'm sure this is costing someone a lot of money." She hung up the phone and stared at it. "How long has this been working?" she asked. "I thought the guy had to come out next week to hook it up."

Tyler and Travis looked at each other and shrugged. "Don't know."

China sighed.

"How did you end up calling Australia?" Deedee asked.

"Australia?" one T said to the other. "Cool!" They high-fived.

"Tell me," Deedee insisted.

"We came in here to clean up like you said . . ."

". . . and we thought it would be fun to pretend to call the main orbiter station."

The other T picked up where his brother left off. "Since we thought the phone wasn't working, I just started punching numbers, and when I said into the phone 'Is this the main orbiter station,' I got somebody talking back. I thought, *Wow! This imagination thing works great.*"

"Was this truly, honestly a mistake?" China asked.

"Hey, we didn't know the telephone was working.

We don't even know how to call Australia."

"We do now," Travis said, elbowing his brother.

"Okay," Deedee said. "You can leave the room now. There's nothing more for you to do here."

The boys ran into the hallway and screeched to a stop. China thought she could almost hear their brakes lock.

"Em! Give me that!" one T said. He yanked a miniature man from the girl's hand.

"Tyler!" Deedee said, taking a chance on the name. "Don't yank things from someone's hand."

"Oh," Emily said sweetly. "Was that yours? I had no idea."

China watched Emily through slitted eyes. Something didn't ring true here. "Emily, do you have the beauty parlor stuff?" China asked.

Emily nodded.

"Then take it downstairs and wait for us there."

"You're gonna play *beauty parlor?*" Travis asked.

"Yes," China said.

"I wouldn't," Tyler warned.

"We know that," Deedee said.

China closed her eyes a minute and pressed her fingers to her temples, willing her headache to leave without a fight.

"Hey," one of the boys said, watching China, "my mom does that all the time."

"Hmmm," Deedee said, "I wonder why."

"She said she's praying for wisdom," Alice said, coming up behind them, her arms loaded with towels and shampoo bottles.

"Your mom has the right idea," Deedee said. She looked at China and winked.

China knew what she was saying. *Why haven't we prayed yet? We talk about what kind of parent God is, but we've never even asked Him what to do here.*

Okay, God, China prayed silently, *can You help us gain these boys' respect?*

By the faraway look on Deedee's face, she knew Deedee was praying, too.

CHAPTER THIRTEEN

CHINA SAT ON THE BLUE-COVERED SOFA with Vickie on her lap. Deedee sat next to her with Valerie.

"I get dibs on the princess hair," Alice shouted, standing behind China.

Emily's expression darkened.

"Oh, good," Deedee said, trying to make Emily feel better. "I was hoping Emily could be my beautician."

China put her hand on Emily's arm. "You're lucky. Deedee's hair is so much prettier than mine."

Emily's eyes suddenly focused on Deedee's hair. A slow grin spread across her face. "I can fix her hair real good," she said quietly.

"See?" China responded. "When things don't go your way, it actually can be better than what you wanted."

Deedee's eyes narrowed. "Are you talking to Emily or to yourself?"

The cat curled into a soft circle on the other sofa, watching the beautification through heavy-lidded eyes. Romeo perched on the back of the couch and made little chirps. As the afternoon sun filled the room with light, China felt the heat go through her whole body. Her mouth, dry and parched, longed for something cold to drink, but she didn't dare disturb this peaceful group.

She kicked off her shoes without a thought about whether or not her hot, sweaty feet were aromatic. Amelia hopped past, gave an exuberant buck with her hind feet, and zipped around the room at great speed a few times before disappearing.

The boys thumped through the house on their way outside with the dogs following them. At this point, China didn't care if the boys got lost, found bears, or went swimming with their clothes on.

Alice started to brush China's hair, and China thought she'd melt into the floor. There was nothing she liked better than to have someone play with her hair. She tried to read the simple board book to the twins—a story about a child who goes shopping with her mother—but her eyes felt heavy with calming pleasure.

Alice got out her bottles and made noises as if she were really squirting the shampoo on China's hair. She squooshed the imaginary shampoo through China's hair, then rinsed it in an empty tub filled with imaginary water.

China could feel the nubbies from the old bedspread making indents into the back of her legs. With each motion of Alice's hands on her hair, China felt more and more relaxed. Her brain purred like the curled up cat on the green couch. Her eyes drooped, and tension left her muscles.

Alice chatted away about how she was shampooing, then rinsing, then drying China's hair. She brushed and brushed to be certain to get out all the tangles. And then she was quiet. The brushing came slower. "I want to use the scissors when you're done, Em," she told her sister.

Emily snipped in the air around Deedee's head. Deedee didn't seem quite so affected by the ministrations to her hair. She read *Go Dog, Go* with such feeling that Vickie began to lean away from China toward Deedee.

Alice rounded the sofa and looked China in the eye. "I really don't feel so good."

"Do you want to lie down?"

Alice shook her head. Suddenly, her eyes flew open. She coughed once and heaved. The contents of her stomach now lay in splatters about the hardwood living room floor. The sofa caught drops, as did China's bare feet. Her shoes fared much worse, becoming canvas bowls for the foul-smelling stuff.

China's stomach lurched, and everything turned dark.

Alice heaved again, and Emily took off, her feet thundering on the stairs. They could hear her bedroom door slam shut.

"Do something, China!" Deedee shouted.

China remained frozen, saying, "I can't."

"What?"

"I hate . . . I . . . can't . . ."

The doorbell rang. Vickie and Valerie seized the opportunity to climb over the back of the sofa and run to the front door to fling it open.

"Gampa!" Vickie called to the old man standing there. "Gampa! Gampa!" Valerie shouted, jumping up and down, clapping her hands.

Vickie grabbed the man's hand and tugged. The old man, dressed in polyester gray slacks and a white button-up shirt, walked in, looking startled.

Deedee came up to him and said, "Hi, I'm Deedee. The baby-sitter for the weekend. Nice to meet you. As you can see, we have trouble here. Can you please take care of your girls while I help Alice?"

The old man looked at the chaos and dumbly nodded his head. He set down his valise and took the girls by the hand. "Do you have any bubbles?" he asked them, slipping easily into the grandfather routine.

"Yeah!" Vickie shouted. Both girls dragged him toward the kitchen.

China felt so gross. She didn't know what to do. She'd always hated vomit. It terrified her. Sometimes she could hardly go on roller coasters if she thought about someone getting sick on them. And in flu season, her biggest fear was that she'd catch the bug and end up hanging over the toilet herself. There was nothing in the world worse than throwing up.

"China," Deedee said, "go wash off in the downstairs bathroom."

China walked around the back of the sofa, then stopped and gasped in horror.

"China," Deedee said, "you can do it. Keep going."

China shook her head and pointed at the floor.

"I'll clean it up. I know you can't do it. If you're going to be such a bum, I'll do it. But go clean up so I can take care of Alice."

China started to cry. She bent over and picked up long curly strands of dark red hair and held them up for Deedee to see. Deedee dropped Alice's hand and slowly reached up to the back of her head. She turned around and China could see hunks of hair missing as if someone had mowed Deedee's head midskull.

"Emily," Deedee huffed. "I'm going to *kill* Emily."

Alice started to cry.

Deedee scooped up the barfy kid and marched upstairs, while China slowly walked through the kitchen to the downstairs bathroom. She could see that Grandpa had the girls entertained outside, chasing bubbles.

China sat on the bathroom counter and stuck her feet into the sink. She turned on the hot water and let it cascade over her pink skin, scrubbing and rinsing three times with soap. When she was done, she went out on the rear doorstep and sat down. She put her head in her hands, willing herself to rid her brain of that awful picture replaying over and over in her mind. Every time she closed her eyes, she could see Alice's face, and her mouth opening. . . . China rolled her head, feeling woozy.

Travis and Tyler zoomed past her into the house. A split second later they were back outside.

"Crud! What is that awful smell in there?"

China put her fists to her eyes. "Alice threw up."

"Cool, can we see?"

China shrugged. "Go ahead. But if you get sick, you clean it up."

The boys trooped inside, appearing a few minutes later. "Wow, she really did the place up good, didn't she?"

China didn't answer.

"What's all that hair?" one T asked. "Did Emily get hold of a doll that hasn't been scalped yet?"

"She's done this before?" China asked.

Both T's nodded.

One said, "Mom won't let them play beauty shop anymore. Em cut Mom's hair once, and that was the end of that."

"She wants to be a lady who cuts hair," the other T said.

"That's why we wouldn't play beauty parlor . . . well, one of the reasons."

"Who's that old guy?" Travis asked, pulling his finger from his ear.

China looked up at him. "What do you mean?"

"You know," Tyler said, "that old guy playing with Vickie and Valerie."

"Don't be funny," China said, going back to pressing her eyeballs. She thought of the houseboat, the cool lake water spraying against her as she skied. She thought of laughing with new friends, telling stories, listening to theirs, sleeping under the stars while the boat rocked her to sleep. *What a screwy trade-off this was!*

"Look, dude!" Travis said. "Male life forms approaching."

"Way cool," Tyler said.

China squinted her eyes at the two boys in the distance. "Deedee's brothers," she announced, wondering what they might add to the present three-ring circus.

"She's got brothers?"

"Yeah, your age."

"Super magna cool."

China waved at Adam and Joseph, then waited for them to reach her. "Hi, guys," she said.

The four boys nodded at each other.

"Can you hold on a minute?" China asked.

Joseph and Adam nodded.

China went to Grandpa and put her hand on his

arm. "Thank you so much for helping. I have a huge favor to ask you."

He smiled at her.

"Have you ever cleaned up vomit?"

Chuckling, he said, "My fair share."

"Uh, I know this is really an awful thing to ask, but could you help by cleaning up after Alice? It's getting close to dinner, Deedee's brothers came by for something, and we could really use all the help we could get."

"This is rather unusual . . ." he started to say.

"Please!" China begged. "This day has been worse than you could imagine."

He looked her over. "Okay. Point me in the right direction."

China showed him where she'd left the Lysol and bucket. She told him where he might find a rag or a towel and sent him inside. She gathered the little girls and gave them each a plastic shovel and bucket she found by the side of the house and set them in the dirt next to the stoop.

"Who is that guy?" one of the boys asked again.

"I'm not in the mood," China warned. She hurriedly introduced the boys around, not wanting to suggest they get to know each other. She didn't want Deedee's brothers picking up anything from these wild boys.

"What did you need?" China asked the visitors.

"BT called," Adam said.

Joseph nodded, his eyes wide and bright.

"He did?" China's spirits immediately picked up and took a dive at the same time. She was disappointed that she hadn't been home to take the call. "What did he want?"

"I guess they're going to be filming an episode up north somewhere—like San Francisco?" Adam said, looking at Joseph. Joseph nodded. "Yeah, San Francisco. And he wants to talk with you about it."

Tyler and Travis looked from the boys to China. "Film what?"

"*Family Squabbles*," Adam said. "I guess it's a TV show. We don't have a TV, so we've never watched it."

The twins stared at each other, mouths open. "*Family Squabbles*? That's our favorite TV show!"

"Oh, yeah?" Adam said. "Our friend BT is on that show."

"BT? You mean—?"

Adam nodded. "Yeah. The guy who plays Johnny Foster."

Travis and Tyler now had eyes the size of saucers. Their heads swiveled in unison toward China. "You know Johnny Foster?"

"Uh, BT, yeah. He's fun," China said with a smile, remembering the crazy nut.

"And you're baby-sitting us?" Tyler's face and voice were full of admiration.

"*Trying* to baby-sit you," China said. She swatted at a mosquito buzzing around her face.

Adam stuck his hands in his back jeans pockets. "And Dad said that there's some guy who wants to talk to you and Deedee about the bears."

Travis and Tyler exchanged glances and said, "What bears?"

"The bears that China and Deedee brought into camp. Didn't they tell you?" Adam asked in amazement.

Travis and Tyler shook their heads.

"Yeah, these bears came and attacked my baby sister. One took part of her scalp off. China saved her life. First she pounded her fist on the bear's head. Then she carried my sister through the forest to the doctor. There was blood everywhere. It would have been cool if it hadn't been my little sister."

Tyler dropped to the ground. "Wow," he said breathlessly, looking at China with new eyes. "Wow."

Travis looked over his shoulder toward the woods. "There really are bears out there?"

"We tried to tell you," China said.

"And you saw them?" Tyler asked.

China nodded. "One too many times. We left food out for them. And that's very dangerous."

The twins looked at her in awe.

Deedee opened the back door. "Oh, hi, guys. What are you doing here?"

Tyler and Travis turned their awestruck faces toward Deedee. China thought they were going to bow down to her.

Adam gave her the message about BT, and Deedee's face lit up.

"One bright spot in a dismal weekend," she commented.

"Oh, yeah. And Mom wanted to know how things were going over here."

Deedee and China exchanged looks.

"It's almost over," Deedee said with a sigh. "I think we can last until tomorrow morning."

"How's Alice?" China asked.

"Sleeping with a bowl next to her. She fell asleep talking about the Coke with no bubbles. Emily is hiding somewhere. Grandpa is in there cleaning up. I almost kissed him for that."

"Grandpa who?" Tyler asked.

"Your grandfather," Deedee said.

"That's not our grandfather."

"You'd better be kidding," China said.

Travis shook his head and said, "Honest. I wouldn't lie about that."

"Then who is he?" Deedee asked, her voice quivering.

Travis looked at Tyler. Tyler looked at Travis. They both looked at Deedee. "We have no idea," they said.

China could swear her heart stopped beating.

"Watch the twins," she told the boys, as she and Deedee vanished into the house.

CHAPTER FOURTEEN

"I'M SORRY ABOUT YOUR HAIR," the old man said, as the girls hesitantly entered the living room. He took the soiled water out front and dumped it into the bushes. When he returned, he said, "That's the third load. I think I've got it all now."

"Thank you so much for helping." Deedee smiled her smile reserved for adults. "But who are you?"

"I'm the Welcome Wagon representative. We representatives visit all the new residents in the area. I have coupons, maps, and free samples to introduce this family to all the services here on the mountain."

"Why didn't you say something?"

The old man smiled. "I tried. But then you looked like you really had your hands full. I didn't think it would be a problem if I helped."

"I don't know how we can thank you," Deedee told him.

"I guess you could leave my card for the lady of the house and have her call me when she returns," he said.

"We can do that," Deedee said.

The old man washed up, then gave Deedee her strands of hair and a catalog. He walked with a jaunty step out the door, closing it behind him.

"Dinner," China said, trying to settle her queasy stomach. "We've got to make dinner."

"Macaroni and cheese, and hot dogs," Deedee said. "I'm glad it's something simple."

Adam stuck his head inside the back door. "Mom said we couldn't stay." He let the door slam.

China opened the refrigerator. Brown liquid dribbled down the drawers and shelves, pooling on the bottom of the refrigerator. A tall slender bottle with the label "Oriental Dressing" stood almost empty. The lid was nowhere in sight. Small sticky fingerprints made a design all over the bottle. China lifted it and sniffed. Sweet. She put her finger to it and tasted. She closed her eyes and handed the bottle to Deedee.

"Coke without bubbles."

Deedee tasted it. "No wonder she lost it. I'd urp too if I drank this stuff like Coke."

China stuck her head out the door. "All right, guys. We've had a tough day. We need some tough guys to help out in here. Do I have any volunteers? Or do I need to use them as bear bait?"

Each boy scooped up a little girl. "We'll wash their hands first, okay?" one T said.

"Yours, too," China told them.

"Okay."

China looked at Deedee, her eyebrows raised. Deedee shrugged. "We'll take whatever cooperation we can get," she said.

China brought out the milk, hot dogs, and butter. Deedee found the box of macaroni and cheese. She put water in two saucepans. While they waited for the water to boil, Deedee ran upstairs to check on Alice. China brought out relish, ketchup, and mustard and set them in the middle of the table.

The animals meandered through, sniffing the air and hoping for a handout.

When the boys returned with the little girls, China said, "One of you entertain the girls. The other set the table with paper plates, napkins, and spoons."

China couldn't believe how they went to work. It was like she had different kids in the house.

She still wondered where Emily had gone. She wanted to hang her up by her toes. She wondered what Deedee wanted to do to her.

China read the directions on the back of the macaroni and cheese box again. She measured milk and margarine into a glass bowl. *So!* her mind prodded her. *Does this Emily thing sound familiar? Have you ever wanted to get back at your mother for not spending time with you?*

China felt heat creep into her cheeks. She'd never done anything so drastic as cut someone's hair off. But she had looked at her mother as someone who had strange thoughts and ideas that needed to be corrected. After all, some of the stuff her mom thought was downright stupid! And so she corrected her—loudly and sometimes meanly.

Deedee walked back into the kitchen. China watched her fingering the ruined back of her hair. It looked awful.

"Do you think Emily meant to ruin my hair?" Deedee asked quietly.

China felt her own shame flood her. "No," she said, shaking her head. "I bet she just thought your hair would look better her way."

"Yeah," Travis agreed. "She imagines she's the world's best makeover artist. She loves those things in the yucky magazines other women give my mom. She always stares in the mirror and wonders what she would look like if they gave her a makeover."

Deedee looked at Tyler. "Do you know where Emily goes when she's in trouble?"

"At our old house, she always went to talk to the turtles."

"Thanks." Without another word, Deedee slipped out the back door.

Tyler watched her. When the door closed, he turned to China. "Whaddya think she'll do to Em?"

"I have no clue," China said. "She had such beautiful hair."

China dumped the macaroni into the boiling water

and set the timer. The hot dogs went into the other pan. "Seven minutes until dinner's ready."

"Can I go?" Tyler asked.

China nodded. She sat at the table, thinking. This day was longer than any she'd ever experienced. Longer even than her frightening flight to the States from Guatemala. She wondered if there was a point to this mess.

She noticed that God didn't necessarily make things nice when you did the right thing. She wasn't sure she liked that about Him. But God was God, and nothing she could do would change who and what He was. She could only accept or reject who He is, not who she wanted Him to be. She knew she could complain all she wanted about the way the weekend had turned out, but it wouldn't change how God handled things the next time.

God's way is not the easy way, but it's the best way, China said to herself. She stared out the dining room window until the forest faded and she could see only what was in her mind. Every single time she had done things her own way, stuff went wrong. On the worst side of things, bears bit little girls. It seemed like some people, like Heather, got away with things. But did they really? Down the road was there a price to pay?

The kitchen timer went off. China turned off the stove and called the kids to eat. They held hands and prayed; the boys prayed that Deedee wouldn't kill

Emily, even if she was a brat. When they lifted their heads, they could see through the large window Deedee walking toward the house with her arm around Emily. Emily had muddy streaks down her face. Deedee walked her to the bathroom and helped her clean up. The boys hardly said a word as they wolfed down their food while stealing glances at their sister to see if she bore any damage on her body.

"Can we be excused?" Tyler asked, his mouth full of a hot dog end.

Deedee looked at Emily, who ate her food without an upward glance. Deedee sighed as if what she had wanted to happen hadn't. "I guess so," she said.

Emily helped Deedee clean up after dinner. China took the little twins upstairs for yet another bath, and Alice woke up and decided she was hungry after all. China sent her downstairs to talk with Deedee. Just looking at Alice made China shake. She wished she could just tell herself to get over it. Fears were so stupid!

After dinner China and Deedee tried to figure out something to entertain the four older children. They didn't want to use the messy crafts they had brought with them. Coming up with nothing, they decided that a bath would take up time. Besides, the bathroom had seen so much grunge that day that it wouldn't hurt for it to see more. In short order, the middle girls eagerly plunged into a bubbly tub. The boys were sent—grumbling and complaining—to their parents' room to shower.

"Aww, do we have to?" Tyler asked for the fifth time.

"If you don't," China said with a smile, "we'll just have to come in and help you like we do the little girls."

China and Deedee had never seen boys move so fast. They sat in the hallway, leaning against opposing walls, listening for sounds of trouble.

"I told you we shouldn't do this baby-sitting gig," Deedee said.

China looked at the floor. "I know you did."

"Well, China honey," Deedee said, in an attempt to imitate Magda's voice, "you can at least learn a lesson from all this."

"I'm 'lessoned' enough for one summer," China told her.

"It builds *character*," Deedee said.

China swiped at her. "I don't want any more character. I want fun."

Deedee looked at China's bare feet. "What happened to your shoes?"

"The Welcome Wagon man probably dumped them in the trash." She wiggled her toes. "I'll just have to toughen these babies up until I can get some replacement shoes."

Alice and Emily called out that they were done, then both appeared wrapped in towels. Deedee offered to help Alice.

Emily looked at China, her eyes large and pleading as China knelt down beside her.

"Did you tell Deedee you were sorry?" China asked.

Emily nodded, and drops of water flew from her wet hair.

Deedee quietly moved away, her arm around Alice.

China tugged on the towel, pulling the back of it up a little to catch the water dripping off the ends of Emily's hair. The remorse on Emily's face stole away China's anger. "Did you mean to hurt Deedee?"

Emily whipped her head back and forth, and China ducked away from the flying water. "I saw this real pretty girl in a magazine," Emily said, "and her hair was yucky long and when they cut it, it was so pretty and nice and I was mad because I wanted to do your hair and I didn't want to do Deedee's until I remembered that picture and I thought she would like it."

"You can't make decisions for other people, Emily. If Deedee had wanted her hair short, she would have it short."

Emily hung her head. "That's what she said, too."

"Are we still friends?" China asked.

Emily looked up at her. "I want to. But you were so busy I thought you didn't have time for me either."

"Friends, like mommies, can't be there all the time, whenever you want them to. Lots of times they're doing other things to take care of you." China sat back on her haunches. "Em, it's going to be a long, hard lesson to learn. Look at me. I'm 15, and I'm still learning that lesson."

Emily smiled really big. "I'll go get dressed myself." She turned red. "I'm old enough to do lots of things myself. I just get lonely, I guess."

China touched the tip of the little girl's nose. "Read, make friends, help your sisters, but don't let your loneliness turn you into a meany."

Emily twirled around and skipped happily to her room, while China went downstairs to look for her shoes.

She found them on the front porch next to the upturned bucket. Both smelled strongly of Lysol. She waited on the porch until Deedee came down.

"The girls are tucked in," Deedee said. "I called to the boys to show their sparkling clean faces to us before they went to bed."

A few minutes later, the boys tumbled down the stairs, hooting and punching one another, trying out karate kicks in the air. They leaped, one at a time, landing next to the girls on the front porch.

"So here we are!" one T announced. "We don't have to go to bed this early, do we?"

Deedee shook her head. "Not as long as you can remain civil."

"I think we can do that," the other T said. "To prove it, I'm Tyler."

Deedee nodded. "Okay."

China decided to ask some questions. If they were going to be civil, maybe she could do some research.

She had to figure things out. Why do people do what they do? Are there consequences for their actions? Why in the world did God put them here this weekend? Or were they supposed to go on the blessed ski trip but missed out because they were too eager to help Magda? She took a deep breath, knowing she might just get them into deeper water. "How come you guys were such jerks in the beginning?" she asked.

Tyler shrugged. "You guys looked like nerds."

"Yeah, like substitute teachers," Travis added. "It's our role in life to torment substitute teachers."

"Why?" Deedee asked.

The boys looked at each other, signaling information.

"It's just fun," Travis said.

"Some of the stuff we don't do on purpose," Tyler said. "We're just having fun. We don't think it's going to make anybody mad."

"But it usually does," Travis said. "We're always getting in trouble."

Travis stuck his finger in his ear, as if it helped him to think. "We like to experiment with stuff. To see how things work. And stuff breaks when it doesn't want to do what we want it to."

"So what made you change today?" China asked. "It was like all of a sudden you were normal boys. A little toady, a little violent in your play, but not wacko."

"Hey. You've seen bears. You've even pounded one that's attacking."

"And you know a TV star."

"Our favorite," Travis said.

"I don't know," Tyler said. "It's like you guys started looking older."

"Or smarter."

"Or something."

Thanks, God, China thought, smiling. *Thanks for the respect—a boys' kind of respect.*

Deedee leaned forward eagerly, eating up all that these boys revealed to her. "Why do you make girls scream?" she asked. "Why do you torment them?"

Tyler grinned from ear to ear. Travis scrunched his mouth up as if trying not to let his smile show.

"They torment us," Tyler said.

"But we get in trouble for it," Travis said. "It ain't fair. They have these high, whiny voices. And when they scream, it sounds like someone's getting killed. When we yell, it sounds like the other way around. So either way, we get in trouble."

"You didn't answer me," Deedee said. "Why do you torment them?"

Travis blushed a little. "It's fun. I'm bigger. I can make them scream."

"Do you realize how mean that is?" Deedee asked.

"We don't mean it to be," Travis said in defense.

"It's not fun for the girls," China said. "It feels awful."

The boys raised their eyebrows. "Oh," was all they said.

China wondered if their words had even soaked one millimeter below the boys' skin. But maybe, if they stopped the boys from tormenting the girls just once, they had done a good thing.

China scrutinized their faces. "So did Emily really make the mess during nap time?"

The boys' expressions took on the solemnity of truth.

"Yes. She does stuff like that so we get in trouble," Tyler said.

"That's why we pick on her the most," Travis said.

Deedee shook her head. "What a little sneak."

"The invisible child really doesn't want to be invisible," China told them all. "She wants to be noticed. She might start acting a little better if you treat her nicer."

The boys rolled their eyes.

"Thanks a bunch for clearing things up," Deedee said.

"If you baby-sit again, we promise not to be so awful," Tyler said.

"At least not on purpose," Travis added.

"Thanks, guys," Deedee said. "We'll keep that in mind. Good night."

"Night."

CHAPTER FIFTEEN

CHINA WANTED DESPERATELY TO GO TO BED the minute the boys went inside. But she knew she and Deedee had to keep awake somehow until they were certain everyone was asleep.

Deedee clasped her knees and looked out toward the trees. "Did you put the bunny in the hutch?" she asked.

"Yeah. And Romeo is in his cage, covered with a towel." China leaned against the porch post. She closed her eyes and turned her face toward the fading sun. It didn't feel so hot and penetrating anymore. It had lost its fury. *Kind of like the terror of baby-sitting six kids. It's exhausting, it's nuts, but it doesn't have the fury it used to.*

Deedee interrupted China's thoughts. "Knowing how much money you earned this weekend, would you trade it for the weekend on the houseboat?"

"In a heartbeat," China said, and turned to look at Deedee. "You were right, Deeds. I'd rather have fun than face something tough . . . or earn money."

"I was just mad when I said that," Deedee said.

"You were right."

Deedee leaned her head back and closed her eyes. "I would trade it, too."

China slugged her.

"Ow! What? You think I'm stupid? You think I enjoyed this insanity? I would much rather have sunbathed with gorgeous guys and been a bum than chase kids all day. No wonder my mom wants my help so much. She's probably hanging on to her own sanity by a thread. Can you imagine living like this day after day?"

"No, thank you," China said. "I think I'll shut my imagination down for the day."

"I'll have a little more respect for Mom after this," Deedee said softly.

"Will you watch the sibs now?" China asked.

"Don't push it. And if you tell my mom what I said here, I'll kill you, then deny I ever said a thing."

"At least your sibs aren't as wild as these," China said. "This whole family doesn't make sense."

"No crazier than you are," Deedee teased.

"At least I'm not as incomprehensible as God is," China said, feeling pouty about how everything had turned out.

"You think He doesn't make sense?" Deedee loved conversations about the real God, not the one some people liked to preach.

"From my point of view, He doesn't," China said.

She tipped her head back to watch the cat walk by on the railing overhead.

Deedee played with the butchered part of her hair. "Why?"

"Look at Joseph," China said. "Every time I hear that story, I wonder why Joseph even stuck by God. Every time he turned around, things were going wrong."

"But in the end it was all that stuff that trained him for what God really wanted him to do," Deedee reminded her.

China sighed. She reached for the cat and set the soft, furry creature in her lap. "I know that," she said gently. "But that's what's so nuts. Why couldn't God just make Joseph the way He needed him to be? Why did he have to be thrown in a well, falsely accused of rape, and stuck in prison forever? Sheesh. I'd rather not have the lessons, thank you very much."

"Me neither," Deedee said. She watched the dogs roll around in the dirt, snapping at each other, obviously having a grand old time.

"Jonah had to sit inside some stinky fish until he came around," China said.

Deedee took the cat's face in her hand. "You would have liked that, wouldn't you?" She looked at China. "He disobeyed, though."

"True. But if he wasn't following God in the first place, he wouldn't have ended up in a fish. Do you see this pattern here? If you want to follow God, there's no guarantee your life is going to be easy." The thought made China slump a little. She felt defeated. She stroked the purring cat, glad something was soothing, even if only for the moment. "I thought doing things God's way got you rewards."

"Maybe the rewards aren't the things we would choose."

"You're starting to sound like my mother. Or yours," China accused.

"Hey, I'm just trying to figure things out along with you. I'm not preaching." Deedee gazed beyond the dogs. Her eyes glassed over. She began to speak slowly, her eyes still seeing beyond the dogs. "The neatest people I've met at Camp Crazy Bear are sometimes the people with the life stories that are the worst."

"But isn't that mean of God?" China asked. "Why should we bother if things are just going to be tough?"

"I don't know. It seems like life is tough whether you know God or not. I don't know. Sometimes it seems like the difference is that God doesn't waste anything."

"A recycling God! How environmentally correct!"

"I mean, maybe this weekend wasn't supposed to be this awful. But God can do something with it anyway." Deedee lost the faraway look. "At least that's what I'm told."

"Do you believe it?"

"I don't know." Deedee crossed her arms and

looked solidly at China. "I reserve the right to make that decision later."

The cat stepped off China's lap, stretching each leg individually. She moved serenely to the panting, resting dogs and sniffed each in turn, then trotted away.

China pressed her fingers to her temples. The headache was on its way back. "I want to go to bed and sleep for eternity," she said.

"I'll get the dogs," Deedee offered. "I'll meet you upstairs."

China snuck a peek in each of the kids' rooms as she went by. All were sound asleep. Except Alice. After all the sleep she'd had from a double nap, she lay bright-eyed on her side of the bed. She had a stack of books around her.

"Will you read me a story?" she asked.

China nodded. She read *Goodnight, Moon* and then tucked Alice in. She kissed her forehead and said a prayer. Then she sang a little song while stroking Alice's wiry hair. By then, Alice had droopy eyes. It wouldn't be long before she slept.

Deedee was already in bed, trying to keep her eyes open, when China came in. China changed into pajamas, brushed her teeth, fell into bed, and was asleep as soon as she turned out the light.

⮥

China woke to a buzzing alarm on Deedee's side of the bed. She reached over and popped the button, then slid out of bed. After putting on her clothes, she went to the little twins' room and got them up and changed their diapers.

The other children came out of their rooms, rubbing the sleep from their eyes.

"Hey, dodo brain," one brother said to Emily. He poked at her with some sort of stick.

"Quit it," Emily said. "Or I'll tell."

"Enough," China said. "Let the poor girl wake up."

"Then we can torture her?"

China ignored the question.

"Where's the other one?" Travis asked.

"She's still sleeping. Come on, I'll get you breakfast."

China padded downstairs to make sure breakfast was done right this time. Cereal in the bowl. Milk in the cup. No food fights.

While everyone ate, Deedee staggered into the kitchen and flopped onto a chair.

"What's with her?" Tyler asked.

"I'm not a morning person," Deedee said with a groan.

A click sounded in the front door. The kids looked at each other. "Mommy's home!" Alice shrieked.

She took off, her cereal spoon clattering to the floor. The other kids followed, shouting and shrieking. China and Deedee held their ground, too tired to go anywhere.

They could hear Alice's voice over everything else.

"The Coke had no bubbles, Mommy. And fish don't like Jell-O. I barfed. And then I ate dinner."

China wondered if the parents listened to Alice any better than she had.

Mary and Pete Macon walked into the kitchen, kids hanging off their legs and arms.

"The baby-sitters are still here," Pete boomed. "The first set we haven't killed."

"You should have warned us," Deedee moaned.

Mary smiled sweetly. "We needed you too much," she teased, obviously thinking Deedee wasn't serious. She peeled a couple of children off her, gently pushing them toward their seats. "Really, though, it wasn't that bad, was it? I told you they're good kids."

China almost blurted the truth. All of Saturday passed before her eyes as if she were about to die. But if God wanted her to learn to control her tongue, maybe this was the time to do it. Besides, this was a great chance to use *discretion*. She decided to let Deedee speak.

"We're usually bored when we baby-sit," Deedee said. "But we weren't this time."

China stifled a choking sound.

"I don't know how you keep up," Deedee told Mary.

Mary smiled. "It's a full-time job, but I love it."

You'd have to, China thought.

"We did have a couple of things we should probably tell you about," Deedee said, sitting on the sofa. Mary and Pete followed suit.

"We encourage our family to have imagination," Mary said.

"I have no problem with imagination," Deedee said.

Except with mine, China thought.

"I simply felt a couple of imaginative turns were rather . . . well, dangerous." Deedee went on to gently tell about the power tools and the fire airplanes.

Mary's face blanched.

Pete's firm mouth drew an even firmer line. He sighed deeply. "I'll talk with the boys," he said.

Deedee looked at her hands folded in her lap. "We had one more tragedy," she said. "I'm afraid the fish didn't live through the weekend."

"Must be the trauma of moving," Mary said to her husband.

"I think we'd like to clean up and get going so you can take care of your family," Deedee said diplomatically.

China and Deedee went upstairs to gather their things.

A deep voice followed them all the way to the back bedroom. "That blond one sure doesn't talk much, does she?" A quiet space followed, then came the booming voice again: "They can't hear me; I'm talking softly."

The girls burst out laughing.

"What are you going to do about your hair?" China asked.

Deedee fingered the shredded ends. "I don't know."

"You won't cut it off, will you?"

"No. I'll either keep my hair in braids or get it layered so you can't tell so much."

China smiled devilishly. "I heard that Emily knows how to braid."

Deedee swatted at her.

Moments later, the doorbell rang and Pete's voice bellowed, "Can Magda come up? She especially wants to talk to China. I told her you don't talk much. I don't understand why she's laughing."

"Send her up," China called.

Magda didn't climb stairs quietly. She thumped and huffed and puffed. She came into the room and hugged China.

"Where's Deedee?" she asked.

"In the shower."

"Why is she in the shower?" Magda asked. "Aren't you going home?"

"She didn't take a shower after Alice threw up on her, and I told her I wouldn't go anywhere with her until she took one."

"Kids." Magda chuckled and sat on the bed. "Well, baby-sitting wasn't so bad, was it?"

"It was *horrible*," China said. "I thought the day would never end."

"Now, don't you go exaggerating like that."

China shook her head, saying nothing more.

"I know those kids can be pistols. But they're good kids. Just like you and Deedee."

Now that's a frightening thought.

"I wanted to come and apologize again for hanging up on you. I was so angry I almost spit across the room. I didn't want to say anything that would hurt our relationship for good, so I hung up. That doesn't make it right, but I did want to explain."

China felt her eyebrows raise. She tried to think of something wonderful to say. All that came out was, "Okay."

"Kemper came by yakking about that ski trip you missed," Magda continued.

"What happened?" China asked. She crossed her fingers, hoping Magda had terrible news to make them feel better about not going.

"Those kids had a ball."

"Nothing bad happened?" China asked, hearing an edge to her voice.

"The weather was perfect, the water was warm, the skiing was great, and the food was terrific—although I don't know how that could be possible, since I wasn't the cook. I guess it was even a low tourist weekend. It couldn't have been better. Well, now, I wish I could stay and say hi to Deedee, but I'm off to church, and I don't want to be late."

China closed the bedroom door feeling sick to her stomach. She continued packing her clothes as

Deedee came out of the shower.

"Magda was here," China announced.

Deedee looked at her, waiting for the news. She gently rubbed her wet hair with a towel. China swallowed, wishing she'd kept her mouth shut. Now she wanted desperately to tell a lie. She sat on the bed to stretch the dried and crusty tennis shoes onto her feet.

"Tell me," Deedee said.

"I can't," China squeaked.

Deedee stood over China. "I'll get the scissors. No, I'll get the power drill. Maybe I'll get Alice to barf on you. . . ."

"Okay, okay. It's like this. Remember what I said about God making our weekend better than the ski weekend?"

Deedee nodded. "Theirs was awful? The boat broke down? They all got sick?"

China shook her head. "Let's just say I was really, really wrong."

"I'm going to get you, China. I swear it."

"I think I'd better go home to Aunt Liddy now," China told her. She got up, grabbed her duffel bag and started to run out of the room.

"Oh, no, you don't," Deedee said, reaching out and grabbing for her arm. "I've got five more weeks to torture you. And I want my money's worth!"

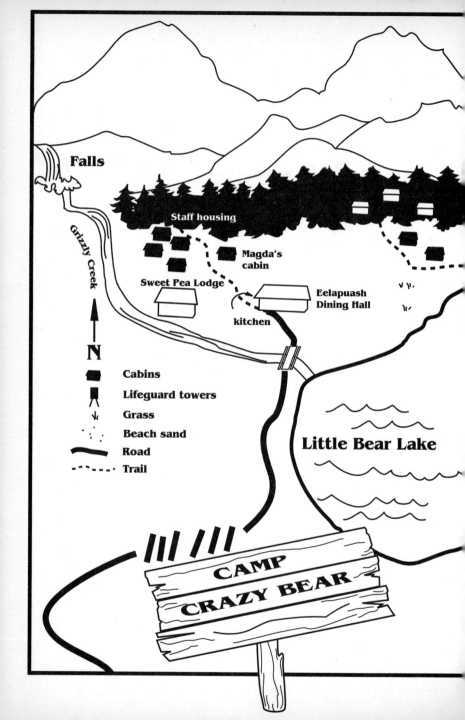

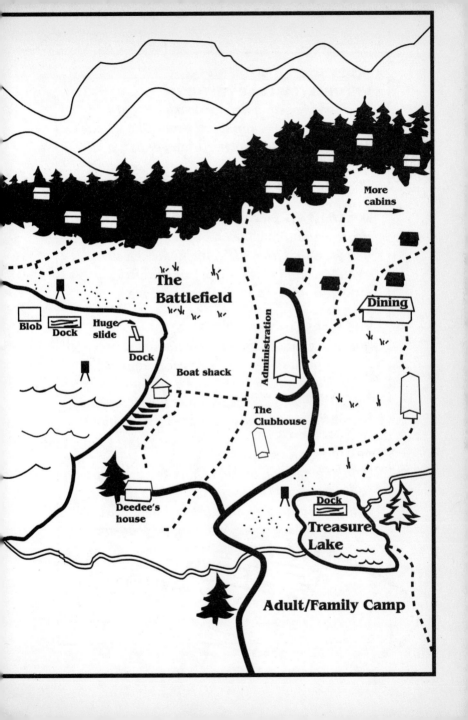

DON'T MISS CHINA'S FIRST SIX UNFORGETTABLE ADVENTURES!

There's more action and excitement as China adjusts to life at Camp Crazy Bear. Although she's enjoying her independence, China finds that getting herself into trouble is easier than learning the biblical truths God wants to teach her.

SLICED HEATHER ON TOAST (1)

Heather Hamilton, the snobby camp queen, has it in for China from the moment they meet. It soon turns into a week-long war of practical jokes, hurt feelings and valuable lessons.

THE SECRET IN THE KITCHEN (2)

After becoming an employee of Camp Crazy Bear, China and her friend, Deedee, adopt a stray, deaf dog . . . even though it's against camp rules. Meanwhile, someone's planning a devious scheme that could cause great danger to China!

PROJECT BLACK BEAR (3)

Thinking it would be fun to have live bears for pets, China and Deedee set out food in an effort to lure the animals into camp. But these are wild California black bears, and the girls' good intentions have disastrous results.

WISHING UPON A STAR (4)

When China discovers that the new kid in camp is actually Johnny Foster of the hit TV show "Family Squabbles," she dreams of a glamorous Hollywood lifestyle—at the expense of her friendship with Deedee!

A COMEDY OF ERRORS (5)

China and Deedee overhear a terrible plot to murder another camper. But what the two imaginative girls don't realize is that the "murderers" are actually fiction writers! Attempting to be heroes, the girls learn a valuable lesson about eavesdropping and jumping to conclusions.

THE ICE QUEEN (6)

China and Deedee have their hands full as camp counselors—especially with Heather, the counselor in the tepee next door! Through some character-building situations like ant-infested sleeping bags, an ice-sitting contest, and getting caught in a mud slide, all three teens learn the value of friendship.

Available at your favorite Christian bookstore.